CONTEMPORARY AMERICAN FICTION

GLASS PEOPLE

Gail Godwin was born in Alabama, grew up in Asheville, North Carolina, and received her doctorate in English from the University of Iowa. She has taught at Vassar and Columbia University and has received a Guggenheim Fellowship and the 1981 Award in Literature from the National Academy and Institute of Arts and Letters. Her short stories, essays, and articles have appeared in numerous magazines and newspapers and her highly praised books include *The Odd Woman*, *The Perfectionists*, and *Violet Clay* (all available in Penguin Books), *Dream Children*, *A Mother and Two Daughters*, *Mr. Bedford and the Muses*, and *The Finishing School*. She currently lives in Woodstock, New York.

GLASS PEOPLE

GAIL GODWIN

PENGUIN BOOKS

PENGUIN BOOKS
Viking Penguin Inc., 40 West 23rd Street,
New York, New York 10010, U.S.A.
Penguin Books Ltd, Harmondsworth,
Middlesex, England
Penguin Books Australia Ltd, Ringwood,
Victoria, Australia
Penguin Books Canada Limited, 2801 John Street,
Markham, Ontario, Canada L3R 1B4
Penguin Books (N.Z.) Ltd, 182–190 Wairau Road,
Auckland 10, New Zealand

First published in the United States of America by
Alfred A. Knopf Inc. 1972
Published in Penguin Books 1986

Printed in the United States of America by
R. R. Donnelley & Sons Company, Harrisonburg, Virginia
Set in Caledonia

for Williamson

GLASS PEOPLE

1 THE BOLTS AT HOME

Her husband folded his arms over his chest and rocked
back on his heels. One newspaper had called this gesture
"the slouch before the strike." But he would never strike
at her. No, he was about to make a significant observation,
that was all. He swayed slightly, a tall skinny figure in
dark, well-fitting clothes, back and forth on the royal blue
carpet, gazing down at her, his eyes slightly narrowed,
his lips pressed together. She knew he was amassing the
precise words he wished to use.

"You are not your old dazzling self, Francesca," he said. "I want you to go somewhere and revive. I want you splendid again."

"Where should I go, Cameron?"

The single object hanging on these pale walls was a large oval mirror. It was tilted at an angle which caught and centered her as she leaned dreamily against the cool leather of the black sofa. She saw herself from where she sat, her mist of dark hair blending with the sofa. She had been called beautiful for so long the words meant nothing. He had come in and caught her sleeping again. She slept a lot these days.

"Why not go and visit your mother? You could call her now and arrange it. You two are old friends, and in your present state it might be best to have a familiar destination. Holidays are stimulating. You may meet some new person, have some new experience, something may happen to make you," and he held out his palm to her, slowly uncurling the long fingers, "open out like a flower."

But his tone of voice killed the flower, made it clear that he thought opening out like a flower was droll, perhaps inferior. He would never do such a thing himself. In the early days of their marriage, four years ago, before her energy drained away, she would dress up and go down to watch him wither his opponents in court. It was better than a movie, he was deadly. He was District Attorney. The papers used respectfully chilling adjectives before his name: *relentless*, *inscrutable*, sometimes *terrible*. *The terrible Cameron Bolt.* Now he wanted to be Attorney General. Recently cartoonists had begun drawing bolts all over the place: arrows, lightning flashes, locks on doors and gates, the crucial part of a firearm. She had never known there were so many kinds of bolts.

He was right, she was not her old, dazzling self. She must get herself together, dress up, go out with him again, help him with his future. But she was always tired, had been for months. She could never seem to get the smallest thing done. Cameron had sat down with her and made her a chart. If she followed it, she could accomplish everything a wife should do and have time left over. But she never could follow it.

"When you said *some new person,* did you mean I should have an affair?"

"You are your own woman," he said. "As for myself, I don't believe in infidelity, but your private life is your own."

What did that mean? He continued to stand above her, perfectly at his ease, swaying a little, watching her. She could see the back of his neck in the mirror.

"I guess I could go and telephone Kate now," she said tentatively.

"Yes. I think you should. Give my best to her, as always." He watched her leave the room.

She went into their bedroom and lay down on the bed, languidly dialing her mother's number in a city on the other side of the country. How long had it been since they'd last talked? Six months? Where had the time gone? A winter and a spring had slipped by her, part of a summer as well, while she had drowsed on the bed and the sofa.

The operator intercepted the call. "What number did you dial, please?"

Francesca repeated the number.

"One moment, please." A silence. Then, "That number has been disconnected."

"What? Is there another number?"

"No Ma'am."

"But why would it be disconnected?"

"I really don't know, Ma'am."

"Well, thank you," said Francesca, a little afraid of operators. She hung up.

"How strange!" she called out, and waited for Cameron to come. There was no answer. He didn't come.

"Cameron?" No answer. He must have gone out again. He often went out without telling her. He slipped in and out like a shadow, unannounced.

What happened to Kate? Francesca tried to remember her last letter. Had it been strange in any way? When had the last one come? She considered getting out all her mother's letters from the last year and going through them, but the effort was too much. The letters were scattered, anyway, some in drawers, others between pages of magazines, wherever Francesca had left them after reading them when they arrived. Had Kate moved? Was she sick? Had she . . . Francesca decided she was being melodramatic. "I'll write her first thing tomorrow, perhaps nothing is wrong, perhaps the phone is just out of order," she said aloud to the immaculate room which she had done nothing to create or maintain. The early evening was filling it with a cheap pink, a color Cameron would never tolerate in his decoration scheme. She hated California. She hated its colors, its gaudy smells and sounds. Synthetic Garden of Eden. She went out seldom these days. Her body was an unhealthy bluish pale (even though that stupid feature in the Women's Section had called it "alabaster"). Cameron played golf. His long, skinny face and arms and hands were a deep yellow-brown. The rest of him beneath his elegant clothes was dead white like herself.

A year after their wedding, Francesca's rich stepfather had been killed. He had crashed his helicopter into the side of a mountain during a thunderstorm. Francesca flew east, to comfort her mother. Cameron had written Francesca laconic letters on his yellow scratch pad paper, including advice and encouragement to Kate: "Tell K. she shall, like Jack Benny, remain eternally 39. My advice is, let her sell what she has, as J.C. urged the rich young man to do, and come to Calif. and be a fisher of men."

Francesca showed these letters to Kate. "Please come," she begged, having reasons of her own for wanting her old confidante near. "Please come and live in California. You could get a great house near us and we could be together every day."

"I wouldn't think of it," said Kate. "Me, a 'mother-in-law'? I wouldn't dream of it."

"Oh please," Francesca pressed. "I want you so much. We could talk every day like we used to. There is so much I need to talk about with you now. Give me one *good* reason why you won't come. It isn't as if you had any ties here. I mean . . ." Then she had stopped, seeing the tears in Kate's eyes. She had thought at the time the tears were for the missed Jonathan, the likable, magnetic little step-father who wouldn't wait for thunderstorms to stop.

"I'll give you one good reason," Kate had said. Then she said, "No, I won't." She wiped her eyes with a handker-chief, and left the room rather fiercely.

Francesca had flown back to California reluctantly. She was perplexed by Kate's behavior. In the months that followed, Kate wrote regular, cheerful letters on her customary heavy beige stationery. One day an envelope arrived with the printed mountaintop address neatly x'ed out. "I have sold the house," the letter said. "It was too big and I got lonely. I have moved back to town, among my enemies. I have a very good apartment, near to town, so I can walk. There was absolutely no need for the Peugeot, so I sold it to a nice automobile mechanic who smoked a cigar. It is so amusing, the way Daddy's old friends who disapproved of me and Jonathan patronize me when we meet. Shaking their heads, hardly able to contain their glee, like Job's comforters."

When Francesca received this particular letter, she tele-phoned Kate at once. "Is there a money problem? You must say. Cameron will help you."

Kate had sounded distant. "I have everything I need," she said. "I have my fur coat, my de Markoff creams, my jewels, my freedom, and my health. I will be extremely upset with you, Francesca, if you mention anything to Cameron. You haven't mentioned anything to him, have you?"

"No, but I was going to. Whatever else he is not, he is

moral, he is dutiful. He would want to help, if there was anything . . ."

"Let him save his morals and his duties for you. Francesca, I want you to listen very closely. Are you listening?"

"Yes."

"If you ever mention anything of the sort to him, you and I will stop being friends. I will feel it, you know how intuitive I am, and I will cut you as quickly and definitively as those old biddies cut me when I married Jonathan. Do you understand?"

Francesca said she understood.

Since that conversation, there had been a distance between the women that far exceeded any geographical one. It was a distance of hearts, imposed by the proud independence of one on the respect and love of the other.

The next day, alone in the apartment, Francesca wrote to Kate. Even in her great concern, it took all the energy she had to find a pen, some paper, something to bear on, and take these materials back to bed, where she wrote slowly, propped on pillows.

Dear Kate,

I telephoned you yesterday and learned that your phone had been disconnected. Is anything wrong? I am trying not to imagine the worst. It seems impossible that so many months have passed since we talked. I don't know what has happened to me. I have lost all my energy. There is no life in me and the days drift by, one exactly like another. The seasons are all the same, you can never know for sure what month it is, no leaves fall or change, this place is like a garden under glass. Cameron is worried about me and wants me to take a vacation. He suggested himself I come east and see you. I could stay about four weeks. He is thinking of running for atty. gen. and needs me alive again. PLEASE let me know as soon as you get this if I can come. I could take that flight that changes in NY and gets to you in the afternoon. I don't think I have ever needed to talk to you so badly. I am unhappy and don't even know why. I need you to tell me.

Love,
F.

She put her raincoat on over her bra and panties and went out and mailed the letter. Back in the apartment she dropped the raincoat on a hall table, knowing Cameron would hang it up later, and padded listlessly about the apartment, opening and closing the refrigerator, stopping to gaze blankly at herself in the oval mirror in the living room. Cameron would not be home for two more hours. What could she do till then? She was not hungry, not particularly sleepy, but she had no energy. Suddenly she remembered the tweezers and went off at once to the medicine cabinet. She got them and returned to the bed. She leaned back on the pillows and crossed one long, pale leg over the other knee. She studied it. It had been two days since she had last tweezed and the hairs were just beginning to return, tiny dark blades tipping up toward the light, barely breaking the skin. If she waited one more day, she could get a better grip on them. But what would she do today? She decided to pluck just a few. With a feeling of anticipation she extricated the first one, just below the kneecap. She held it between the tweezers and looked at it. There it was, root and all. A little white nodule, like wax. Proof of life. Or was it? No, hair grew after death. At a party with Cameron once, someone had told the story about how Jean Harlow's mother would bring a hairdresser regularly to her daughter's grave.

"Well," drawled Cameron, "Did you manage to write your letter today?" He was slouched over the kitchen counter, in his shirt sleeves, tossing the salad greens. He was as cool and crisp as the lettuce. Francesca sat at the table, making patterns on the frost of her martini glass. She had spent the remainder of her afternoon dressing for dinner, after the tweezing. Cameron did not mind cooking or setting the table, or even washing up, as long as she sat across from him looking perfect.

"And mailed it, too, you'll be amazed to hear."

"Good girl. You can do things when you want to."

After dinner, over coffee, he said, "Don't frown so. Preserve your beautiful forehead. You'll feel better soon. It does a young wife wonders to go home and talk about how terrible husbands are with her mother."

"Don't say that."

"Why not?" He raised his flat gray eyes to her. The irony suddenly went out of them and she saw how serious he was about her. "I know I don't please you, my love."

Tears rolled down her cheeks. She did nothing to stop them.

"I'd like to help if I could," he said.

"I'm a disappointment to you," she said. "I'm not the wife you hoped I would be. You are so cold to me."

"You are wrong," he replied quietly. "You were and are and always will be the wife I want, the wife I need. As for my being cold to you, I don't think you really believe that. Don't project your feelings onto me."

Francesca began to cry. She knew it was true. "Please don't give up on me," she said, watching the tears drop and spread on the tablecloth. Now why had she said that?

He wiped his lips, folded his napkin, and came around to her. He took her napkin out of her lap, dipped a corner of it into her water goblet and bathed each of her eyelids. He smoothed her heavy hair away from her face with his hands.

"Francesca. Let's go to the bedroom."

She rose without a word and accompanied him. The tears stopped. The bed looked a mess from her afternoon in it, writing and tweezing. She hoped he would not be angry. But he was not looking at the bed.

He undressed her slowly, folding each garment and laying it on a chair. He touched each piece of her clothing as though it were very delicate, very valuable. At last she stood naked before him. This was the part that terrified her, when he knelt in front of her, still fully clothed himself, and kissed each of her bare feet, then let his eyes travel slowly, very slowly upward, inspecting inch by inch of her. As a collector might go over a piece of precious sculpture, examining it for chips or flaws. At such times, she thanked the fates for her beauty, she needed every bit of it. A woman a fraction less beautiful would have died under that cold, passionate scrutiny.

At last the eyes finished her face. Had she passed the test again? She had.

A rapt expression on his own face, Cameron said in his slow voice, "Go and get ready, my dear . . ."

Off she went to the bathroom, to cope with jelly, springs, and rubber. She took her time because she knew he liked to be undressed and under the sheet before she returned. He was self-conscious about his skinny body. She rinsed her hands and gazed in the mirror. It had often crossed her mind that Cameron disliked her using a diaphragm, would have liked to make her pregnant, even, except for the fact he did not like her to stay in the same room while he undressed.

Afterwards, she asked, "Do you ever wish we could have a baby, Cameron?"

Characteristically, he switched the question back on her. "Do you ever wish such a thing, Francesca?"

"No. Not really." She looked sideways at him. He was lying very stiff and straight under the sheet, a slight faraway smile on his face. His reddish-gray hair was damp against his forehead. He had acne scars on his hollow cheeks and at the jawline. He looked very faraway, very self-contained. She often had the urge to shake that composure, shake it till it rattled, maybe fly out at him from the bathroom before he finished undressing, catch him just stepping out of his shorts . . . but she would never dare. To make up for this blasphemous thought, she now said, "But sometimes when we're making love I think I wish it . . . I don't know why, it's very funny . . ."

"Why is it funny?"

"Oh I don't mean funny exactly, I mean odd. It's as though I want some final force to enter me and take over my body, set me on some genuine destiny that can't be changed, that I can't turn back from. Oh, I can't explain it, it's weird."

He shifted his position, propping his face on one hand so he could look at her better. She could tell he was interested. Then suddenly his face changed. He swore and reached beneath him and held up a small glittering object.

"Oh God. I'm terribly sorry."

Her tweezers.

"What, pray tell, were you tweezing in bed?" he asked, massaging himself beneath the sheet. She was scared to death she was going to burst out laughing. He would never forgive her for that.

"I might as well tell you," she said, deciding her safest course was to collude with him against her own foolishness. "It's my secret vice."

"I see." He handed her back the tweezers with great courtesy. He looked censorious.

"What I do is pluck out the hairs on my legs one by one. See?" She lifted a smooth leg up for his inspection. If only she could make him laugh. "It's my project. I get a great sense of accomplishment from it. It's my form of housecleaning. Since there is nothing else that ever needs cleaning around here. I can do it for hours, as long as the hairs hold out. I only wish there were more!"

His face had gone from censoriousness to mild alarm. She didn't want to alarm him, only to make him laugh.

"You know that old wives' tale about two hairs always coming back in place of the one? Well it's false! Only one comes back. I speak from experience. What a project I'd have if they did multiply. Then, the next time one of those women from the paper came to interview me, to do a story on Mrs. Cameron Bolt at home, I'd have something to tell her. 'What are your special interests, Mrs. Bolt, do you sketch or do embroidery or throw pots or—' I'd smile mysteriously, and say, 'Actually, I'm a devotee of pluck-ing . . .' "

Cameron was not amused. He reached across to the chair by the bed where his black silk wrapper had been laid in readiness. He whisked this around himself as he got out of bed. "Perhaps you ought to go back to school," he said.

"Or a job. I could get a job."

"A job? How on earth would you ever get yourself to-gether to go to the job, Francesca, not to mention per-forming its duties? What you need is a vacation. Away from those—tweezers. And away from me too, perhaps." He went into the bathroom and turned on both bathwater taps full force. She heard the faint rumbling sound which meant he was emptying his bowels. He always ran the water first. His public image was maintained scrupulously, even in the privacy of his home. After his bath, he emerged and began laying out fresh clothes.

"Where are you going?"

"To the Brewster dinner. Remember?"

"But you already ate dinner."

"I don't like to gorge myself at these things," he said and selected a scarlet-and-lime striped silk tie from his crowded rack. "Would you like to come with me? You were invited."

"I can't cope with parties just now. After I come back I'll be better, I promise. I'll dress up and go to everything with you. There will be hundreds of people saying clever things tonight. They won't miss me."

"I will," he said. He slipped his black-stockinged feet into a pair of patent leather pumps. "A beautiful woman is her own excuse for being. You don't have to carry around a trunkload of repartee, Francesca. The less said, the more mystery. I've told you that." On his way out he stopped to pat her arm as one might take leave of a tiresome invalid. "See you tomorrow." He left.

Francesca could not move. She needed to go to the bathroom, but continued to lie motionlessly upon the sheet dampened by their exercise in lovemaking until the pressure on her bladder forced her to get up.

She woke. Was it morning? She heard Cameron washing the dishes in the kitchen. Through the closed bedroom door, she could hear "Jesu, Joy of Man's Desiring" on the stereo. She was thirsty and considered calling out to Cameron to bring her a glass of orange juice, but somehow didn't want to interrupt the orderly sounds of organ music and clinking silverware. Besides, he couldn't hear her with the door closed. Had he closed the door when he left the room? What time was it? She got up, slipped on a dressing gown, and went blinking into the living room. Light was everywhere. All the lamps were on. Their white globes stung her eyes. The apartment glittered and shone: its wax surfaces, its metal surfaces, its lacquer and marble surfaces. It frightened her more than usual, this exquisite setup, no more than one or two colors allowed in any room, furniture straight, bare, unobtrusive, fitting into its corners like bunkbeds aboard some sleek ship. All walls were cream, all trim was black lacquer. The chairs and couch were cream and black leather respectively. The color in the living room was one: royal blue. The royal blue wall-to-wall carpet. Francesca walked hurriedly through, as though unsure of her right to be there. The kitchen was white, black, aluminum (sinks and canisters) and yellow (refrigerator, stove, and curtains). She leaned on the door frame and watched Cameron, looking absurdly innocent and happy, for several moments before he saw her. He was wearing her tie-around apron over his trousers and her yellow rubber gloves, which did not quite come to his wrists. He was doing the glasses now, swishing each one in the fresh sudsy water, then rinsing it and holding it up to the light with the pride of the man who might have blown it. He rocked back and forth on his heels, his toes turned outwards, his nonexistent stomach poked forward beneath the frilly apron, and Francesca began to smile, bordering on a laugh, when he turned and saw her.

He raised his eyebrows.

"I was thirsty," she said, not smiling now.

With great care, Cameron selected one of the clean glasses, ran cool water in it to take away the steam, then went to the yellow refrigerator and poured ice water into it. He handed it to her as though it were a glass of champagne.

She drank while he stood in the gloves and apron watching her.

"I didn't hear you come in last night," she said.

He raised his eyebrows and gave a little smile. "Didn't you?"

"Was it fun, the dinner party?"

"Amusing." He took the large sponge, soaked it under the tap, squeezed it thoroughly, and began wiping the surface of the kitchen counter, the edges of the stove, though they looked perfectly clean to her.

Francesca sank down in a chair and leaned forward on the formica-topped table. She bowed her head and watched the thick strands of dark hair weave back and forth across her vision. Too much light. There was too much light in this room. Why not open the curtains and let the sun in, turn off these harsh lights? The Bach was getting on her nerves. The repetition.

"Would you like some orange juice? I've squeezed some fresh," said Cameron, his back to her, swabbing around the handle of the refrigerator now.

"You must think I'm a pig," she said, her head bowed low, her finger tracing doodles on the table top. "I should be the one washing the dishes, squeezing the juice."

He didn't answer. She heard him select another glass, rinse out the steam, open the refrigerator again, and pour liquid from one more pitcher. A yellow-gloved hand offered her the glass of freshly squeezed juice.

She sipped it. It was delicious. "Why are you wearing those gloves? Men don't wear rubber gloves when they wash dishes," something made her say.

"Most men don't wash the dishes," he replied.

"Oh Cameron, I'm sorry. Why do you put up with me? Why do you do all my work?"

"I don't mind doing any amount of your work, Francesca. I like making things go smoothly. All I want in return is for you to be happy. Drink your juice."

"Why not open the curtains," she suggested.

He looked surprised, but went at once and pulled the cords. The yellow curtains above the sink parted, revealing a square of pitch black night.

"But it's still dark!" cried Francesca. "You said it was morning."

"No, I didn't."

"Well, you let me think it was morning. Oh, I don't know. I do need a vacation. I'm losing my mind."

2 THE MEETING

Her father had died in her eighteenth spring, leaving Francesca and her mother comfortably provided for, if they were careful. Which they weren't. After fourteen months of twice-daily visits to a private clinic where people, including a man they both loved, lay in various stages of becoming corpses, the two women hurried.back to the world of the living with a desperate enthusiasm which shocked the more conservative of Francesca's father's friends. He had been a good deal older than his wife Kate, who had married him at eighteen.

They did not plan ahead. During Kate's first year of widowhood, Francesca left school and they traveled. They spent carelessly, whimsically, and let others do their planning. "I saw an article on Yugoslavia in this travel magazine," Francesca would say. "There was a nice gloomy castle overlooking the sea." So they went to see it.

Everywhere they went they passed as sisters, Kate being boyishly thin with cropped curly hair the color of vermouth, and always laughing, always the wit, her face in perpetual motion, looking years younger than her thirty-seven, and Francesca looking older than her teens because of a certain finished quality about her features which was often mistaken for the kind of serenity which comes with self-knowledge and maturity.

Francesca was very beautiful. People stopped on streets and turned to gaze back at her. She haunted people, even her own mother. Kate would steal looks at this statuesque creature with the deep-set, heavy-lidded eyes and the rather swollen, childish upper lip, the graceful stemlike neck and the dreamy way of walking, moving. Is this really my child, Kate would think, this lovely sleepwalker? Should I wake her and warn her of the exigencies of reality? What are they? Do I know them myself? So she continued to let her daughter be, her own brisk, smartly shod steps echoing beside Francesca's dreamy ones. Let her be, Kate decided, not without jealousy: she has only to keep still and some man will always come and save her.

The two women talked a lot. Francesca was deeply impressed with Kate's fund of woman's lore. Francesca had just reached the age where her attention was centered upon the mysterious rituals of being a woman, how to preserve and enrich the spell, how to taper the flame to a mere suggestive gleam, or focus it—like a mirror catching the sun—till somebody went up in flames. They discussed styles of sensuality. "My style is light-hearted, rather formal," Kate said, "like being discreetly drunk on chablis in a garden of pale roses. What is yours?" "I see mine as darker somehow," said Francesca, "but I can't express myself like you do. What do you see mine as?" Kate closed her eyes and considered: "Like . . . rich, ripe globes of fruit hanging passively in a dark night . . . and tempting some sharp-eyed thief." The two women broke up with laughter, then went out to buy gloves.

How they spent money! They collected silk scarves and jewels, handmade shoes and exorbitantly expensive handbags, suitcases big and little, perfumes, cosmetics, negligees. They bought as though for a campaign, as though they had sighted a moth already circling and circling, nearer and nearer to their irresistible twin flame.

Jonathan really did fly into their lives, landing his helicopter on the green sward of Kate's May-wine party, a year and a week after the death of her husband. A friend of some new friends, Jonathan was a short, neat little man with a delighted laugh. Everything about him was as quick and creative as a sleight-of-hand. He gestured madly when he talked, his small fingers skimming the air, shaping it, plumping it up, and rearranging space like a pillow. He could not enter a room without moving something, somebody, re-creating the environment in some way. Everyone said he was fantastically rich, had interests in this corporation, that wild scheme, but nobody put a finger on exactly what Jonathan did. He went here and he went there, always piloting himself, driving himself, he could not stand to sit back and wait for someone else to take him there at their own speed.

He was a Jew. This fascinated Kate and Francesca, neither of whom had even had a Jewish friend. In that small conservative community, whose sophistication did not extend beyond its boutiques and Little Theater, he was somewhat of an anomaly. This increased their respect for him: the two women were coming to think of themselves as "liberals" compared to those prudential friends, contemporaries of Kate's late husband, who frowned on her frivolous widowhood. They did not feel she was raising her daughter in a suitable atmosphere, out-of-towners buzzing in like fireflies to May-wine parties, all that gaiety and satiety. A few "well-meaning" women told her so. Kate tossed her head and told them sweetly where to get off. They cut her in return, but, as Kate laughingly told Francesca, what a relief to be spared those bridge parties.

Francesca was now a day student at the local college, which was richly endowed in agriculture and science, barely accredited in the humanities. But she didn't care. She chose to stay home, and Kate wanted her to get a college education, so they compromised. She signed up for undemanding courses that sounded interesting: astronomy, art appreciation, theater of the absurd, and spent her evenings talking to Kate in their new mountaintop house.

Jonathan worshipped them both. He was fascinated by

their lore. He adored going shopping with them, he would follow them tirelessly about for hours, sniffing their creams and scents, judging their clothes, finding out why Kate preferred plain beige notepaper to tissue-thin pink with a border of little roses, asking why Kate had remarked of some woman on the street: "No, she's got herself up all wrong." In the car he always remembered to see that the windows were closed to keep the girls' hair from blowing. He bought them presents which showed how carefully he had listened to their preferences.

He had an astonishing network of "connections" and "acquaintances," some of them people he had never even met. During her art appreciation course, Francesca expressed more than her usual passive interest in Van Gogh. Jonathan was overjoyed. He made a phone call and she found herself in Amsterdam at Thanksgiving, living a few blocks away from the museum in the home of an elderly Jewish couple. They treated her like a long-lost daughter. One evening, sitting around their crackling fire, drinking schnapps and watching the lights of the boats on the dark canal below, she asked them how long they'd known Jonathan. Surprised, the man answered that he had never had the pleasure of meeting Jonathan but it was through their very old friend Peter Bern that they had been honored by her visit.

It was not clear which of the two women Jonathan was courting. Kate was certain he was after Francesca. Who wouldn't be with her beauty? Francesca assumed he was after Kate. She herself was not physically attracted to him. He visited them assiduously, took the two of them everywhere, brought them each expensive gifts reflecting equal amounts of thought. One evening Kate said to Francesca: "A man in his early forties, as long as he has kept his vitality, is a perfectly eligible husband for a girl almost twenty."

"Yes," replied Francesca carelessly, "but he doesn't attract me."

Kate burst into tears. Why, she's in love with him herself, Francesca thought.

One evening when Jonathan had alighted on their lawn, Francesca went out to meet him. He remarked how he was falling in love with their mountains and was thinking about building a little place here himself. "That's extravagant," she said. "Why not marry Kate and live in our new house. There's room."

Jonathan gave her a bright, oblique little look. "Do you think she'd have me?"

"Of course."

And so it was done. Francesca sometimes wondered what would have happened if she had said, "Why not marry me and live in our new house?" Jonathan was a cunning operator. But he was a likable cunning operator.

He did move in with them, after some protest. Kate said, "After all, if you were to build me a house, you would build what I wanted, and since I have already done that, what's the use of doing it again?" But Jonathan re-created the house. He made it denser, deeper, moved in his own rich style. He flew in and out of their mountains, attending to his multiple businesses, attending to his women, ascending and alighting in his self-piloted helicopter, a small, neat, slightly balding man, bringing gifts and friends. The old friends of Kate's late husband snubbed her on the street. "The hell with them," she cried, "we've got Jonathan's new friends."

One of these friends was a district attorney from the west coast named Cameron Bolt. "That Cameron! A frightening boy!"

"Does he frighten you?" Francesca asked Jonathan. She had not met Cameron yet. He was due at the house for dinner.

"Me, no. I'm immune. That is why, I suspect, he likes me."

"Tell us why you're immune," said Kate affectionately.

"With Cameron, one has to be either above ridicule or willing to let him find you ridiculous. The persons he goes for are those who have something to hide. Me, what have I to hide? And I don't mind being the Ridiculous Man Incarnate."

"You're not ridiculous!" cried Kate loyally, beaming at the warmhearted man who kept *her* so immune.

"Doesn't he ever do anything ridiculous?" asked Francesca.

"Never."

Francesca shrugged. She went away to her room to dress for dinner. This Cameron was certainly not going to find her ridiculous. She dressed herself austerely, so that her beauty shone out like an affront. "There," she said to the mirror, "take a good look, Mr. District Attorney." She decided to make his evening miserable, and when the bland friend of Jonathan's arrived exactly on time, with his flat little smile, his acne-scarred jaw, his thin shoulders weighted down by his brocade dinner jacket, speaking modestly, deferentially to everyone, she was disappointed.

He did not look very sinister or frightening, he was just a polite, conventional man in his thirties. She retired early, leaving him sipping brandy with Kate and Jonathan.

"That poor man," Kate said afterwards. "You certainly frightened him off. What got into you?"

"What makes you think he was frightened?"

"He told Jonathan so."

"Oh, what did he say?"

"He told Jonathan, 'That is the most beautiful woman I have ever seen, but she is formidable.' "

"I thought he was too thin," replied Francesca, secretly gratified.

Time passed. When school was in session, Francesca drove up and down the mountain, back and forth to school. She made a fourth at dinner parties for Jonathan's other friends and acquaintances who flew in from various places. A millionaire from Venezuela proposed. "I have to finish school," Francesca said. He went away and sent her a diamond that covered the first joint of her fourth finger. She held it up to the light, admiring its fiery opulence, then asked Jonathan if he would wrap it and send it back again. No more was heard from Venezuela.

She was now a senior in college. The three of them sat around the table in their mountaintop house, discussing what she should do with her life.

"Would you like to go to London?" said Jonathan. "I know someone in the Department of Labor there. You could be his secretary, go to all the embassy parties."

"She can't type," said Kate. "Would you like to go to art school, Francesca? Remember how you loved that art course?"

"That was art history, mother."

"I know! Publishing," said Jonathan. "Ted Silvers is a great friend of mine. Would you like to work in a very prestigious publishing house, meet authors?"

Francesca didn't know what she wanted to "do." She was content as she was. She had her own wing in the house, she didn't bother anyone. She liked the leisurely drift of days, where she would sit at her dressing table, brushing her hair, planning what she would buy in town. She liked shopping. She and Kate had made an art of it: the planning and precision, what went with what, textures, lines, cut. She liked the anticipation of it, the satisfaction of it. She liked to see her three-way image making the salesladies happy. "Oh! That dress was made for you!" It was a ritual that fit her like a glove. She understood it. She liked driving her car, just driving off: all the preparations, getting dressed, checking her pocketbook to see that everything was there, then off down the mountains, expectantly, even though she might be going nowhere in particular, maybe to town, maybe not, maybe to feel the wheel take the mountain curves in the elegant little sportscar Jonathan had given her. She liked being asked out by the town's young men: a lawyer, a tennis instructor at a nearby boys' prep school, certain engineering students, students at the college. She drove in her little car to their various apartments or small rented houses and let them make supper for her, frowningly uncork some special wine or other, and afterwards make love to her on various-sized beds, always with fresh sheets. But she was never really able to let herself go. Why was that? Such nice young men, she liked them all, their clean, energetic bodies, their efforts to please her. But all of her lovers seemed to freeze her into an image and hold her there. She gave up her body to them, and yet she felt as though the real Francesca floated somewhere above the two people, bemused by their movements, their urgent attempt at communion, as though she were watching a dance or a fight which must come to an end. She always drove home afterwards, feeling a little sad but not knowing why, eager to get back to her wing of the mountaintop house, where she would drop her clothes on the heavy rug, wander dreamily to the bathroom, her own bathroom with the sunken tub, shake in the scented salts, and brush her teeth or hair until the steam hid her own face from the mirror. In the tub, she would lie back and talk to herself, not moving her lips, but hearing her own voice inside her head. "Such a pleasant person, that X . . . so tender . . . the way he dusted my chair with his linen napkin before he would let me sit down . . . what would X be like as a husband? No, I couldn't imagine him as a husband. Who can I imagine as one? Nobody. Perhaps I won't marry. What will I do? What do I see myself doing? Why do they draw a line at graduation and after that I have to take off like a runner in a race? Why do I have to decide what I am going to 'be'? Well, Kate and Jonathan certainly aren't going to kick me out on an appointed date. Besides, does a person always have to go out and seek destiny? Perhaps my destiny will come and seek me . . ."

Cameron Bolt surprised everyone by showing up for her graduation. He told Jonathan confidentially that he had come for a month or so in these lovely mountains. He needed to rest his spirit, tidy up his soul. He rented a little chalet on another mountain, and Jonathan got him a special guest's pass to the country club golf course. He eagerly accepted all dinner invitations at Kate's and Jonathan's, saying that he was exhausted with degenerate western society and craved solitude except for their company. After dinner one evening, he and Francesca wandered out to the swimming pool. "What is it like to be a DA? Do you frighten people? Are you feared?" she asked.

"I fear you, a little," he replied.

"You fear *me*?" asked Francesca, incredulous.

"A little," said Cameron. Then suddenly his attention left her. He knelt by the edge of the pool in his neat dinner clothes and scooped out a drowning black beetle. He transferred the insect to the grass.

"He'll just crawl back in again," Francesca said.

"Not while I'm around to see it," said Cameron.

She allowed him to take her out. They went to the few good restaurants and Cameron would order wines she had never heard of and suggest what she would like to eat. He took her golfing at the club one day, but she gave up after two holes, let him put his golf hat on her head, and followed him around in the electric cart, watching him play, his flat, rather grim countenance breaking into a smile when he made a hole in one. He heard of a French restaurant opening a hundred miles away and they set out late one summer afternoon and returned after midnight, Francesca wearing his jacket because it had been too pretty a night to drive with the windows closed. She never drove the car with Cameron, he wouldn't let her. He had rented an enormous car, which he drove easily, rather cautiously, never exceeding the speed limit. Francesca leaned back against the spacious front seat, feeling safe, a little drowsy, and listened to him talk. He spoke slowly, precisely, often pausing in mid-sentence till he found exactly the word he wanted. He told wry anecdotes about the foolish things people did, people in court, dim social acquaintances whom he must tolerate in the course of his job. Francesca was a little awed that this man who was so critical of others should find her worth talking to. She folded her arms and smiled enigmatically, pretending to understand more than she did. He did not touch her, except to help her in and out of the car and take her arm when they entered restaurants. His self-restraint created a curious tension in her. She asked herself: is this the beginning of passion?

One evening he invited her to his chalet for a drink. "That would be lovely. I can't stay too long," she said, wondering why he hadn't asked her sooner.

He mixed them drinks. "This is called a White Spider," he said. "Don't drink it if you don't like it. I can always make you something more conventional."

It was clear and minty and very cold. She liked it. However, after his remark, she would have drunk it or died. They sat side by side on the couch. She could not locate many traces of him in this room, some news magazines, his golf clubs. She sipped the White Spider and saw a reflection of her cool, impassive face in the greenish-gray mirrors of his eyes.

"You don't have a lot to say, do you?" he asked.

She smiled and didn't answer. She had a lot to say, to

people like Kate and Jonathan, all those good-natured clean young lovers down in the town, but she cultivated silence when she felt out of her element. She continued to sit, her long bare legs, tanned from days by the mountain-top pool, aligned primly, knee to knee, beneath her short summer skirt. She decided to look at him, something gave her the confidence to do this. She took in his languid posture, the tight-planed, acne-scarred face, the intelligent, rather flattish eyes, and now a little smile. What was the meaning of this smile? What would it be like to kiss him? He had large, clean, square teeth. The left upper front one was black around the gum. This suddenly glimpsed taint of vulnerability inspired her to be daring. She leaned across to him, watching herself for courage in his eyes, tipped his chin as men had often tilted hers, inserted her cold, minty tongue between his lips, which had parted in surprise, and ran it lightly, precisely, around the edges of the dead tooth.

He removed her drink and placed it next to his on the table. Then he sank to his knees below her and embraced her legs. She was immensely relieved she had remembered to shave them today. Amazed, she felt herself stirring, beginning to lose her distance, as this cold, formidable man ran his tongue softly across her knee.

The telephone rang.

Some girl who had agreed to turn state's evidence had tried to kill herself. He had to take the next plane out. Francesca listened to him snapping requests to an airline. He could barely make it to the airport in time. What if the girl died before he'd got her evidence down on tape?

"Now what are we going to do about you?" he said, very

businesslike, all traces of the strange reverent passion gone. "I haven't time to drive you back to your mountain. Shall I drop you in town, or what?"

"I could just wait here," Francesca said. She really did not want to inconvenience him.

"What? I'm going to California. It will be several days before I could possibly get back. What do you mean? Would you really wait for me, for days, like that?"

"Sure. It's nice here. I like it."

He took her by the shoulders and went over her face. What was he looking for? "There's food, of course," he murmured, "I didn't want to be bothered shopping every day . . ."

"I don't eat much," she said.

A whimsical little smile touched the corners of his mouth. "You would really do such a thing?"

"Why not? I've nothing better to do."

"Why not indeed. Stay here then and wait for me. I'll come back as soon as I can and we'll finish our evening." His eyes had already left her face and were ranging somewhere out of focus. She had the queer feeling he had been suddenly, magically, transported to California and what she was seeing was an after-image.

Then the after-image was gone and Francesca was left to wander about the chalet, wondering a little at her own crazy whim. She went to the refrigerator and sampled a few things—all of which she liked: pâté, some Stilton, the remains of a bottle of white wine.

She telephoned Kate. "I'm up at Cameron's. He had to go off to California. Some girl, some prisoner, tried to kill herself and he didn't have time to bring me home."

"I'll come and get you," said Kate.

"No. I'm going to wait here. I promised. It's a sort of game."

Silence. Kate said, "Are you sure you want to play a game with this man?"

"Why not?"

"Well, in that case, we'll see you when we see you. Is there anything to eat at his place?"

"Yes. The refrigerator is full of the kind of things I like."

Five days went by. Francesca slept, took long baths, nibbled from the refrigerator, drank Cameron's whisky, tried and failed to re-concoct the White Spider (how had he made it so cold?) and snooped. She went through his closet and touched his clothes. There was a certain shirt— she took it out carefully and laid it on the bed. It was a subtle shade of lavender, like some skies before a bad storm, with a tiny silvery design in the material that re-sembled wings. The shirt was cut in panels, making the wings go up and down on the front and back, then east and west on the side. She rustled the shirt under the light and a thousand pairs of wings took off in all directions. She smelled the shirt, hoping for Cameron's smell. But the shirt was new. Its synthetic odor was a disappointment.

In the daytime she sat outside on the little balcony which jutted out over the woods. She sat in the shade and noticed, with a kind of curious pleasure, how quickly her tan faded. Perhaps, by the time he got back, she would startle him with her paleness. She thought of women whose husbands went away, traveling, or to sea, or some-thing, how, when these men came back, they would be surprised at some small alteration in the women, some glow or pallor, some difference in the hair, some added plumpness. Thinking such thoughts by the hour aroused Francesca, a little.

One evening she drank too much and went to bed before dark, wearing his pajama top for comfort. She had a nightmare: she was wandering the streets of a large, gray, impersonal city. Nobody turned to look at her, nobody knew her name. Then she began looking at windows, hoping to reassure herself by her own reflection. *But there was no reflection!* She started banging on the windows, trying to attract the attention of people inside. There was a restaurant window, people were busy eating and talking inside. She banged the glass until it might break, and called through the glass. A man and a woman, in a booth just inside the glass, did not even look up. Francesca screamed.

She woke to find Cameron gazing down on her with concern. He was fatigued and rumpled from his journey and looked older than she'd remembered him.

"Oh God. I'm so glad—I was having a nightmare." She raised her arms to him like a child.

He sat down at once beside her and held her face between his long hands, which were cool, and she searched his eyes and saw herself again.

"I should take a bath," he said.

"No, don't."

"Really? Why not?" He seemed amused. With one hand he tugged his tie loose.

"I want to know what you smell like."

"You are a strange woman, Francesca. You baffle me."

"Is that good?"

"Mmm. Yes, perhaps."

"Did you get what you wanted?"

"I don't know. Did I?"

"I mean, the girl. Did the girl die before you got there?"

"No, she didn't. Everything's in order. Why is your forehead so hot?"

"I was having a nightmare. Oh it was so awful. I'm glad you're back. You saved me from my nightmare."

"I'm glad, too."

The extravagance (vulgarity, some insisted) of Francesca's mid-summer wedding to the District Attorney from California was talked about by Kate's critics for a long time afterward. "I'll bet she wished she had the price of that farce he threw for the daughter now," they said. "Flying hairdressers and friends in like circus performers. They were so arrogant up there on their mountain. Money like gold dust. They thought they could outwit natural law. Flying helicopters into thunderstorms."

3   A COOL WELCOME

The envelope was one of the stamped ones you buy at the post office. The postmark was a rural town some fifty miles from Francesca's old home. But that was Kate's typewriter.

DEAR FRANCESCA

THERE IS NOTHING TO AMUSE YOU HERE. I HAVE MOVED AND HAVE A SMALL CABIN, THAT IS ALL. THE NEAREST AIRPORT IS FAR AWAY AND IT WOULD BE DIFFICULT FOR ME TO MEET YOU. I'M SORRY YOU ARE UNHAPPY. ASK C. TO TAKE YOU AWAY.

LOVE, KATE

Francesca re-read this strange, cryptic reply many times. She shook her head, exclaiming aloud, trying to rub some of Kate's old warmth, her old collusion, into it by going over each word again and again. Finally she telephoned Cameron at the office.

"Something awful's happened. She's not herself." Francesca read Kate's letter over the phone.

"What a bore," said Cameron. "We'll have to think of something else for you. It's impossible for me to get away just now. Now more than ever."

"Cameron, do you think she's sick, I mean mentally?"

"No, the letter says she's moved. What was the postmark again?"

"Claretown. It's a little rural town about fifty miles away from where we used to live."

"Mmm."

"Cameron, what do you think?"

"It might be many things. I don't think she's gone mad, though. She might be doing a Walden. So many people are these days. Would you like to visit her in her cabin?"

"Oh, I don't know," Francesca was about to cry. "I don't know if she wants me."

"When was the last time you wrote to her?"

"It was six months or more, I'm afraid."

"Then she's understandably cool. Do this, are you listening?"

"Yes."

"Write her back at once. Say you're sorry for being such a bad correspondent. Say you'd love to come and see her and her cabin. If she still says no, we'll send you somewhere else on your jaunt."

"Oh, I feel so awful. I don't feel like going anywhere. Let's just skip the whole thing. I'll try and do better."

"No. There's a certain point on the spectrum of apathy, and when you reach it you can no longer 'try and do better.' You have to be hurled back into life. Look, do you think you can fix yourself some supper? Nat Kramer and I are meeting to talk about the campaign."

"I'm not hungry. Do you really think I've reached that point?"

"I do, but you can be revived. Write that letter and *mail* it today. When I come home I'll fix you something, if you're still awake."

"That's a pretty safe bet for you. You know I won't be."

"Dear Kate," she wrote, as though Cameron were dictating the letter over her shoulder. "You have every right to be cool to me for being such a negligent correspondent. I'd love to come and see your cabin. You don't have to meet me at the airport. I'll take a bus, hire a car, whatever is necessary. The point is, I want to see *you*." She paused, looked around guiltily, then added, "We shared so much together. *Before* Jonathan, *before* Cameron. There are things I need to share with you that I could never share with him."

Obeying Cameron, she dressed and tramped out into the dry white afternoon to mail the letter. Kate had probably run out of the expensive beige notepaper and was reduced to these post office envelopes. She would bring her more. And a supply of Alexandra de Markoff and other gifts as well. She would win back her mother as a friend and confidante. And Kate would explain to her in those incomparably witty turns of phrase why she was unhappy with Cameron.

A week passed. Francesca slept a lot and plucked her legs on alternate days. Cameron hummed to himself when he was home, which wasn't very often. Late one night he defrosted the refrigerator and waxed the kitchen floor. He needed little sleep. He had the energy of ten people. Now he made up batches of things and left them in the refrigerator for her to nibble at. Gazpacho. Deviled eggs. Chicken salad.

Finally another post office envelope arrived.

DEAR FRANCESCA

TAKE THE BUS TO CLARETOWN. THAT IS THE NEAREST STOP. SOMEONE WILL MEET YOU IF YOU LET ME KNOW YOUR SCHEDULE.

K.

Not exactly a comradely embrace, but not the rejection Francesca had feared, either.

4 CAMERON AWAITS FRANCESCA

Four weeks later, on a Saturday, Cameron let himself into the apartment. He went straight to his study, where he sequestered his golf clubs in a corner of the closet and hung his golf hat on its hook. It was early afternoon and he was savoring this particular slice of time, the hours before he was due at the airport to pick up his wife.

He took off his shoes and ambled into the kitchen in his black socks. He liked the waxed smoothness of the linoleum skidding against his feet. He made himself a drink: a gin and tonic, replacing the portion of lime he did not use in a plastic bag, refilling the ice tray with water, sponging off the few flecks of wet from the kitchen counter.

Drink in hand, he went to the bedroom, stood in front of his open closet, his nonexistent stomach slouched forward, and with his free hand selected his welcome-home outfit for Francesca. He had made reservations at a fine new restaurant for dinner. Of course, he had gone there to sample it first. He'd taken along his faithful secretary, Paula (happily married to a TV scriptwriter), who had been honored and rather touched when Cameron confided he always liked to sample Francesca's pleasures first, to make sure she wouldn't be disappointed. Did Paula think his wife would like this restaurant?

He ran his bath. While it was running, he went back to the kitchen and made himself a chicken salad sandwich on onion rye. He had imagined himself standing here spreading homemade mayonnaise and chicken salad on the bread just like this, even the smooth swish of the waxed floor beneath his socks, while sinking the putt on number 9 this noon. He often did this: projected from one moment into another. The present for him existed frequently as a kind of featureless tower, as close to him as an epidermis, from which he manipulated searchlights over past and future. This way of living in time he had practiced ever since he could remember. It cut down discomfort and increased efficiency. If he was quicker at tasks than others, it was because he had mentally rehearsed them many times, had seen himself doing them hours, days, before he had to do them, anticipated all eventualities. In the act of doing them, he was somewhere else already, rehearsing new tasks. Or perhaps remembering previous rehearsals of the present task. Just now, for instance, as he sank the knife into his freshly made sandwich, he was not in the kitchen at all, but both on the golf course anticipating these hours before Francesca and in the restaurant sitting across from the candlelit face of his newly returned wife, listening to her news while waiting to tell her his own. He was not here at all. This ability "not to be here" was, in fact, the secret of his well-known imperviousness. He never got shaken in court for the simple reason he was no longer there. He had arrived and departed before the others ever came. That bland face they saw was only mouthing rehearsed lines while the mind behind the face was already preempting some future confrontation.

In the bath, he lay back and let the hot water redden his pale flesh, tanned only from the neck up and the elbows down. He imagined Francesca, in the air by now on the last half of her journey. She would be leafing through a fashion magazine or gazing blankly out the window at cloud formations, thinking perhaps nothing at all.

He shaved, considering his face in the mirror. He compared it to a recent cartoon in which the artist had copied Dürer's famous Four Horsemen woodcut and substituted Cameron's head for Death's. "Who Will Clean up after the Apocalypse?" the caption had read. Cameron bared his big teeth and grimaced at himself. That goddam dentist. The black gum irritated him, but the rest of his face did not. The flat cheeks, the prominent jawbones, the thin nose pointed and sharp like an accusing finger, the roughened skin beneath the year-round tan. Some men would not be overjoyed to confront such a reflection in their shaving mirror, but it had not done badly by Cameron. His formidable courtroom presence would have diminished considerably had he been born a jovial endo-morph and reached manhood with his Ivory complexion intact. More than half the population was and always would be half in love with death, and not so easeful, either. A stern retributive figure riding his skinny horse of justice roughshod over their bugbears, that was what they craved. And as their chaotic guilts increased in direct proportion to the freedoms they could not handle, the bugbears would breed like pests. For the bugbears were but their guilts turned inside out, made manifest.

He was an expert on guilt, had observed with interest its cumulative patterns for years. It was a most ingenious phantom builder who needed only one or two scraps of remorse with which to construct a city of endless woe. Give it an inch of concrete shame or self-doubt and it would spin out a four-lane expressway of self-vilification. Give it the tiniest amount of silence and it would fill that silence with a cacophony of conscience-stingings and prickings. If a man's (or a woman's) guilt mechanism was in working order (and whose wasn't these days?) all you needed to do was sit back. Wait. He couldn't stand the silence, the waiting. Soon the old phantom builder would drive him to your door, his (usually overwritten) con-fession signed and sealed. You would take it from 'him, relieve him of the burden, and he would sink happily into

your graces, a willing servant. On the other hand, *if you
refused to take it from him,* the effect would be just the
same.

Cameron patted his cheeks with a stinging after-shave.
He put on clean underwear, re-fastened his watch, and
shrugged into his black silk wrapper. He retrieved the
sandwich from under its napkin on the kitchen counter
and went into his study to read the seven letters his wife
had written him during her month's vacation. As each
letter had arrived, he had dutifully slit it open with the
Moroccan letter opener the court stenographer had
brought him from his holiday. He had skimmed the con-
tents, just to make sure she was doing what he thought
she was doing. To tell the truth, he preferred his wife's
silences. He wished there were more of them. Then her
ineffable beauty shone out and she was his mysterious,
beautiful woman again. Still, Francesca would expect him
to have read the letters and if he read them through like
this, at one sitting, he would capture her chronology of
the trip and impress her with his understanding of the way
she saw things.

The first letter was short and disconnected. Cameron
skipped the plane and bus travelogue. Some new "friend"
of Kate's had met Francesca at the bus station. No more
was said about this friend. Kate had changed. She had a
"new taciturnity." Cameron was pretty sure this new
taciturnity did not keep the two women from discussing
everything thoroughly the first day.

Second letter. In which she was obviously bored to
death but trying to be chatty. Too many details which

meant nothing. Trees, leaves, skies, Kate's garden. The friend, it seemed, was allowed in Francesca's narrative to "help out in the garden" and make himself useful to the women in general. Cameron could see it all from what Francesca left unsaid.

Third letter. Uh-oh. Reminiscence time. Francesca was now dredging up the old, opulent days of Jonathan & Co., how she'd met Cameron that first evening. "Here I was, expecting you to be so terrifying and so I decided to terrify you first." Now why did she have to go and tell him that? He would speak to her when she returned. Not to-morrow, no, let a couple of days go by, let her have time to become sufficiently impressed by his news. Then: Francesca, you are a mysterious and beautiful woman. Why spoil the effect by telling too much. Don't explain your-self. Let people wonder.

His telephone rang.

"Hello?"

"Cameron, you are going to kill me."

"Francesca, where are you?"

She'd missed her flight, she said.

"Ah me," he sighed, suppressing his keen disappoint-ment. She embarked on a confused saga of how she'd gone to the wrong terminal, there were so many at that airport, she'd thought it was an American Airlines flight, the one coming east had been, then when she checked her ticket it had been too late . . .

Cameron knew his wife, he knew every tone of her voice. He knew she was lying.

"Cameron? Are you furious?"

"Of course not. Why should I be? But do try hard to

get the right terminal tomorrow. Can I count on your being on the same flight tomorrow?"

"Yes, of course," she said, too quickly, uncertainly.

"Where will you stay tonight?"

"Oh, I found this nice hotel very near the airport. You can even see the planes in their hangars from here."

"That's very nice." Cameron carefully did not ask the name of this hotel.

There was a pause. Cameron waited, listening with interest to the airwaves between them. He waited for her to fill up the empty space.

"Cameron, I really am sorry to ruin your Saturday. I know how you like things to go according to schedule."

"All the more eager to see you tomorrow, love. Just please don't ruin my Sunday."

"What . . . what will you do tonight?"

"Eat dinner by myself. Re-read your letters."

"Oh you make me feel terrible."

"I don't mean to. It's not your fault you missed the flight. It could happen to anyone. See you tomorrow, Francesca."

"Well, goodbye . . ." She hung on, chastened.

"Goodbye, Francesca."

After he hung up, he took the half-eaten sandwich into the kitchen and dropped it into the trash can. He fastened the top of the yellow disposal bag and took it outside to the incinerator. He returned to the kitchen and re-lined the trash can with a fresh bag. Then he wandered into the bedroom, opened Francesca's closet and studied her clothes for a while, running his fingers softly over various things. He touched a pair of jade green silk hostess pants, which she wore with a perfectly simple white Russian tunic. She was stunning in that outfit. His face went abstracted, rather dreamy, he swayed a little on his bare feet like a man who has lost his balance. He looked down where his black wrapper had come apart and studied the enormous erection. Then he got dressed quickly in clean golf clothes, grabbed his hat, his clubs, and left the apartment.

5 ANONYMITY

Francesca replaced the white receiver in its cradle and shook her head from side to side, as though trying to clear her ears. "Oh, I don't know . . ." she said. She sat on the edge of a king-sized bed covered with a quilted spread of cerise and looked around this room she had never seen fifteen minutes before. It had been furnished—as Cameron's apartment had been—without her suggestions or approval. But she found this room pleasing, the way she might wish to furnish a room herself. The framed prints of birds above the bed. A scarlet tanager. A red-winged blackbird and his mate. The birds were colorful and lifelike in their austere perches. She might have chosen them. At any rate, they were better than no pictures at all. Cameron was the only person in the world she had ever met who did not have pictures on his wall. When she asked him about this, he had said, "I don't feel the need to tack up my personality—or what I want people to think my personality is—on every clean space. I reside *here.*" Tapping his breastbone thrice, definitively. She had heard a hollow sound. Yet another time he had said, "If you don't hang pictures, then people will speculate on the sort you might hang. I like to give them their pastime. That way, everyone is happy."

"Oh, I've got to relax," she said. "Cameron is three thousand miles away. He's three hours in the past. As long as I stay here he can never catch up with me." She leaned back a little and laughed. She liked the cerise bed, the bright birds on the cream walls of this warm anonymous room with its sounds of jets rising and descending . . . so close. The heavy red curtains were slightly parted and through them she looked out across a distance of highway and beyond to a complex of hangars, the wings and up-tilted tails of jets at rest. The air-conditioner purred softly. It was a sunny late-summer afternoon and the light coming through the curtains was a gentle yellow, almost gold. Sleepy yellow and warm cerise.

"I can never tell if I am fooling him or not," she said.

"What did he say?" asked the man sitting in the armchair near the bed, watching her.

"Oh he said, '*Do* try to get the right terminal tomorrow, my love.' And he didn't even ask the name of this hotel, after we went to all the trouble of signing in in my name. A waste of time!"

"Perhaps not. Perhaps he is shrewder than you think. It's possible that, right now, he is calling all the airport hotels, checking to see if there is one with a Bolt listed."

"Oh no, not Cameron. You see, he has this thing about me being my own woman. I can do whatever I like as long as I don't confess to him. What's the matter? Why are you looking so . . . dubious? I tell you, that's the way our relationship is. Oh . . ." She pressed the flat of her hand to her breast. "I can't breathe sometimes, after I've talked to him. He makes me feel full of . . . I don't know . . . fear, something. While *you* . . ." She ran across to him and hurled herself into his lap. He folded her in and kissed each ear. His face disappeared beneath the heavy fragrant curtain of her hair.

"Oh, why am I being so morbid," she went on, "he's not here, he's far, far away. Oh don't stop, don't stop."

"Shhh," he said. He picked her up and carried her to bed.

Outside, the sky changed slowly, moving through an infinite variety of tints. Dark smoke from jets mingled with cloud formations. The room filled with shadows that worked themselves forward from corners. The sky turned its last shade of orange. One star appeared through the small opening in the curtain. The man drew the top sheet over them both and propped himself up on an elbow and lit a cigarette. He carefully blew the smoke away from the sleeping woman, whom he watched until it was too dark to see her face. In California, Francesca's plane skidded noisily to the runway and taxied toward its gate.

6   A NEW KATE

Francesca's hopes for a renewal of the old relationship with Kate were not realized. The old Kate was gone.

She had been met at two a.m. at the tiny Claretown bus station by a large, plump man who introduced himself as Ware Smith. He had a heavy reddish beard and small, twinkling blue eyes, and spoke in a high, jovial voice, announcing himself as sent by Kate, asking Francesca all the expected questions about how many hours she had traveled and if she was very tired.

"Yes, I am," she said, to make allowances for herself while she tried to "place" him. What was his relationship to Kate? Handyman perhaps? He wore a workshirt and overalls, but they were new looking, there was something of the costume about them.

"Gee, I'm sorry to hear it. We have a fairly long drive. It's the Land Rover." He helped her in, then went around to put her bags in the back. It was cool in the mountains and he had thoughtfully left the heater running. Francesca hugged her bare arms and tried to dismiss the probability that had entered her mind.

He got in on his side and off they went. Francesca couldn't start a conversation. What was there to say? She was glad the Land Rover was noisy. It made a monologue of its own. The most casual question from her might elicit an answer she didn't want to hear.

It didn't seem to make him nervous, driving in the dark without talking. Finally, he asked, "Are you hungry?"

"A little."

He reached under his seat and brought out a paper sack. "Here. This will tide you over till we get to the house."

With a sudden vision of one of Cameron's super sandwiches, Francesca reached into the sack. Her fingers encountered a number of small hard things. "What . . . are these?"

"Oh, nuts, raisins, pumpkin seeds. I always carry a little something with me, to keep up my energy."

Francesca selected the familiar shape of a raisin and nibbled it. "How long . . . has my mother lived in this new place?"

"I persuaded Kate to give up the rat race the end of February." This was said quite simply, but Francesca knew he was telling her. Still, she insisted to herself, there were some special circumstances, some mitigating distance between her mother and this Ware Smith. Who was he? What did he do? She was afraid to ask.

"Kate says that you've been down in the dumps. I suppose the weather out there must be hot, humid. No, I guess not, with the sea so close. I always wanted to go to California." He laughed. "Maybe it's not too late."

"It's true, I haven't felt like doing much lately. It's not the weather. It's just me."

"Perhaps you have a B-vitamin deficiency," he said thoughtfully.

They rode in silence.

"Are you a farmer?" Francesca asked.

"I am now," said Ware. "Though, like a lot of people, I've become one out of necessity. I don't mean to say I don't enjoy it. I love it. I love it now. But at the start . . . oh well, it was rough going." He laughed delightedly. "Some of the mistakes I made, you wouldn't believe it! But Kate was grand. She helped a lot. She knew even less than I did and in some way that made me feel like I knew more. Do you understand?"

"I think I do," said Francesca, remembering an important maxim of Kate's lore, one that she had impressed on Francesca often: *When a man is uncertain of himself, never allow him to admit it to you. Pretend you think he's doing marvelously. And he will!* Oh, she was ashamed of not liking this robust, simple man better, but could Kate really have . . .? "What kind of work did you do before?"

"I had a little store. Natural Foods. In the town where you used to live. That's how I met your mother. She came into my store one day, and—" he took his plump hands from the wheel to make a gesture of amazement, "—it all began."

The deep pride, almost worship, in his voice kept Francesca quiet for the rest of the drive. She was busy accommodating herself to this new reality: Kate and a new man, a man so different from her father, even from the witty, sophisticated little Jonathan.

At last, Ware's Land Rover crested a mountaintop and stopped in a clearing of woods. Stars burned in the dark sky. A woman came out of a very small house and walked toward Francesca, who burst out of the car in tears caused by memories of former halcyon days and expectations for a complete reunion. "Francesca!" "Kate!" The two women embraced. Then both withdrew, embarrassed. Francesca was glad it was dark so her mother couldn't see her face as she struggled to cope with a second new reality. Kate was pregnant.

"I'll bring the bags," called Ware's cheerful voice. "You girls go on inside."

"Yes, let's go inside," repeated Kate, not very heartily. "Did you . . . did you have a good trip?"

"Not bad. I'm a little tired, but . . ." Was she really exchanging such tepid pleasantries with *Kate*, the witty raconteur who had once been merciless toward people who resorted to mundane chit-chat to cover up real feelings? Downcast, she followed her mother into the small house. Gone also was Kate's brisk, effervescent walk. This woman ahead of her put her feet down heavily, puffing a little. Francesca wished she were back in California.

"Here we are," said Kate. She let her daughter go first into a rustic room which also served as kitchen. She looked briefly out into the night where Ware was, as though she was getting reinforcement.

"How . . . charming," ventured Francesca, looking around the room. Perhaps she could leave sooner. Arrange secretly with Cameron to be summoned back for some crucial political appearance. It was true, the room was charming in its own way, with its solid, crude oak pieces and the bright dried flowers in large ceramic pots by the fireplace, and all the kitchenware shining on hooks. It was like the room of a houseproud peasant. Or like those rooms in magazine articles, rooms of young people who had dropped out of society and were trying to re-create the pioneer style of their ancestors. But this homely make-do-with-what-we-have, it was not Kate's style, the Kate who went swiftly across thick beige carpeting, her stockinged legs brushing together like soft wind, the Kate who sipped Lapsang Souchong from a paper-thin china cup in bed, her short, vermouth-tinted curls squashed against a pile of pillows, her quick, slim body wriggling beneath its pale satin comforter as she chatted confidingly with her daughter.

"How nice you are," replied Kate. She took Francesca's hand and looked up at her. "My goodness, you are so beautiful, I had forgotten."

"Oh, beautiful!" scoffed Francesca. "Well, you are certainly looking healthy yourself." She hoped she seemed approving of Kate's longer hair, brushed straight to her shoulders, clean and shining but with gray strands showing through the untinted brown; of the robust, glowing figure. She had never realized how short her mother was; formerly she had always worn heels.

"Healthy I am," laughed Kate, looking vaguely off into the room.

Both women were immensely relieved when Ware came in, made them all a bedtime drink of hot milk and honey, and insisted they talk after everyone had gotten their forty winks. Francesca was shown her tiny room, a sort of converted porch which contained a cot piled high with blankets. "Well, Francesca, you'll be the first to use our guestroom," said Ware. "I've put in windows and all, but it still gets chilly, I'm afraid. Still, it's kind of nice to lie in bed and see all the stars."

He and Kate went off to another room Francesca had yet to see. After a cursory appreciation of the stars, she fell into a quick sleep.

She woke early. She'd forgotten how noisy birds were. Ware was clattering about the kitchen, whistling a tune. Something was steaming in a big iron pot on the stove.

"Good morning, Francesca. Did you rest well? Katie's sleeping a while longer, it's her habit now. Do you like oatmeal?"

"Oh, don't bother. Just a cup of coffee is all I need."

Ware shook his head. "No coffee in this house, I'm afraid. Steel-cut oats with raisins, fresh dairy cream, unprocessed sugar, and country-churned butter. We get our dairy products from a wonderful old couple, they live down the hill. Do you know they've lived in these mountains for seventy-nine years, never eaten anything from a can in their life, never had electricity in their house? It just shows you . . . I'm sorry about the coffee, honey, but you'll get used to it. You won't need it after a few days. Just think of all those blood vessels in your brain, shrinking . . . brrrr!"

After breakfast, he loaded the Land Rover with boxes of vegetables, the earth still dripping from them, and drove away to Claretown, to sell them at Farmer's Market. Francesca wandered disconsolately about the room, feeling sluggish from the oatmeal and warm cream and sugar and butter. If she were back in California, she would crawl back in bed with a magazine. But there were no magazines around, and the cot on the porch did not encourage luxurious lieabouts. She tiptoed, listening for signs of Kate. For lack of anything else to do, she wrote a short letter to Cameron on the heavy beige stationery she had brought as a present to Kate, along with the jars of de Markoff cream. She wondered if they would take the jars back.

At last Kate came out of her room. She walked heavily in her smock and sandals to where Francesca sat embellishing the envelope just addressed to Cameron. "Good morning, darling," Kate kissed her daughter's head. "Nice to have you here."

"Nice to be here," Francesca murmured. It was like being stuck on a mountaintop with a stranger. This woman was so different. She moved differently, spoke differently, and her looks were totally altered. Not that she was ugly or anything, most people would find her healthy, rosy-plump dreaminess very agreeable. It was just not the old Kate, that was all.

"Have you eaten? Yes. Would you like some tea with me?"

"I'd love it." Then she couldn't resist adding, "But doesn't it have caffeine? Doesn't it shrink the blood vessels in your brain?"

Kate put a kettle on. She brought to the table a leather box which Francesca immediately recognized. She sat down with a little sigh, across from Francesca, and folded her hands on this box. The nails were short, cut straight across, unvarnished. "This tea," she explained, looking directly into her daughter's eyes, "has *some* caffeine but not as much as . . . the regular teas. I have always had tea in the morning and it is a habit that dies slower than others."

Francesca understood that there was to be no collusion between the two women over the absent Ware. She accepted her tea when it came. Kate opened her old jewelry box and selected two yellow pills, a clear ruby red one, a long creamy brown one, two blue, and a tubular maroon one. "Will you take some vitamins?" she asked. "They're very good for you."

"Sure, why not?" Francesca remembered when they had bought that box in Florence. "What are they, anyway? What's this pretty red one, the clear one?"

"Oh that's gelatin," said Kate. "And these yellow are B-complex, very good for brain energy. And the browns are E, they prevent aging . . ."

"Oh really?"

"Yes, and these blues are A's . . . for eyesight and so on, and this thick fellow is a sort of all-purpose thing . . ."

Their heads were very close together as they examined the vitamins, just as they had formerly inspected Kate's garnet earrings, the diamond brooch, the squarecut emerald Jonathan had given her . . . the Scandinavian silver bangles and the cameos and the cat's eye and the turquoise and sapphire costume ring . . . where were those other jewels now?

After three cups of tea, Francesca said, "I guess I should mail this letter to Cameron sometime. Is there a mailbox anywhere near?"

"Yes," said Kate quickly. "At the foot of our hill. It's about a quarter of a mile, but you'll enjoy the walk."

So Kate, the new Kate, was feeling strained as well.

When Francesca came back from her walk, Kate had gone to her room again. The door was closed and Francesca did not dare to knock. She was relieved when Ware came home.

"Thirty-nine dollars, Francesca!" He came in rubbing his plump hands together. "What have you two girls been up to?"

"Oh we . . ." She started to say "had some tea together," then decided not to. "I walked down to the mailbox. It's very pretty . . . very *wild* around here . . ."

"Very good," Ware nodded. She supposed he was approving of her walk. "Is Katie resting?"

"I think so."

"Well! How would you like to help me get dinner ready? Do you feel up to picking a few vegetables? I'll need a cauliflower . . ."

"I can't tell which vegetable is which . . ."

"Well, come on out to the garden and I'll show you. Then you can do it yourself another time!"

Ware merrily prepared dinner while Francesca sat at the table, her hair falling across her eyes, watching him for lack of anything better to do.

"This must surprise you, my cooking," he said. "A man cooking dinner. But as I told your mother—she felt a little funny about it at first—we have gotten into this role thing, the man has to have his role and the woman hers, and that's just nonsense. I like to prepare food, and Katie's always had servants before, and . . . well, why should some outworn notions keep me out of the kitchen?"

"Cameron sometimes prepares dinner," admitted Francesca, noting the touch of pride in Ware's voice when he'd said that bit about servants. My mother is his princess, she thought.

She went to bed early. Rather, she went to her little porch room and waited for Kate to come in and sit on the foot of her bed and ask about her marriage to Cameron. But Kate did not come. She listened to their voices droning on and on behind the door of their bedroom. What were they talking about? Vitamins? What had Kate suffered down in that town to make her retreat to the hills with Ware Smith? How did such unlikely people get together? Did people choose people or were they driven into relationships? Had she chosen Cameron?

In the mornings, she haunted the little house, waiting for Kate's late rising and tea invitation. Francesca drank cup after cup of the tasteless, watery tea, because this was the only time they came close to talking, while Kate was partaking of this last of her old habits. Perhaps the bit of caffeine and the jewelry box between them provided a kind of magic space through which they could re-enter the past. But it was never enough. Kate would only go so far, then escape to her room.

"How did you and Ware meet exactly?" Francesca wanted to hear Kate's side.

"It was very . . . odd," said Kate, looking into her tea-cup. "He ran this health food store. On Brown Street, remember? Next to all those boutiques. I went in one day. I'd been reading about organic foods and decided I needed to overhaul myself. So I went in and asked him and he was a great help. I went back a week later and he had this book for me. He said he'd saved it for me. It was just a book about nutrition, but I was touched that he had saved it for me. It was a time when . . . well, when a gesture like that went a long way. A long way. After that, he told me how badly his store was doing, though I should have guessed, there was never anybody else in there when I came in . . . and then, well to cut the story short, we decided to pool what resources we had and take care of each other. Since we weren't doing a very good job taking care of ourselves."

Francesca decided the time had come to ask the question. "Didn't Jonathan leave you . . . what happened to Jonathan's money?" She sat back, waiting for a rebuff.

But Kate smiled. It was the kind of smile a mother might give when remembering a beloved dead child. There was no rancor in it. "Jonathan was a fascinating man. He was a magician," she said. "He created the illusion of money. But the illusion depended upon his staying alive. There were . . . quite a lot of debts, you see."

"Oh, Kate! If only you had let me know . . ."

Kate held up her hand. That was enough of that. "I'm all right. And how are you, Francesca?"

"Oh . . ." now that the much-awaited time had come, Francesca could not think how to start. "Marriage has been strange for me. It's very strange. It's a little like being frozen, or hypnotized. Sometimes, I feel as though I am slowly becoming paralyzed. I can sit around for hours and do nothing, see nothing. I feel like I am slowly turning to stone."

"Perhaps the alternative is to let yourself turn into someone else," mused Kate, swirling the tea dregs in her cup.

"Is that what you did?" Francesca pressed eagerly.

Kate got up from the table and rinsed her cup. "I can't answer for you, Francesca. Why not go for a long walk in the woods. The silences will tell you more than I can." She went to her room.

So Francesca began exploring the woods. She was afraid of snakes and poked the terrain ahead with a long stick and wore knee socks. As the days passed and no snakes struck, she let down her caution. She found a small clearing at the top of the ridge and sunbathed, first in her bikini, then in the nude. At first she took the stationery which she had decided not to give Kate and wrote letters to Cameron. It seemed necessary to put something between herself and the woods. She lay on her stomach and pushed the pen drowsily across the paper, describing trees, skies, the forest floor to him. He would skip these parts, but they seemed a crucial prelude to the things she wanted to say. She did not talk much of Kate and Ware, left it ambiguous. She wrote little memories about their meeting, hers and Cameron's, their first times together, trying to recapture how it had been. She wanted to find out at what point she had decided to marry Cameron. Was it before he ever came to dinner, when Jonathan had described him as being frightening? Or had it happened when Cameron said he feared her and then knelt and scooped the beetle out of the pool? Or did it come later, when she waited for him up at his chalet?

The sun poured down through the opening in the woods. She melted a little, felt her pores open, sometimes she felt them breathing, inhaling and exhaling. She began to think of passion. It must be something like this: a slow warming of yourself, inch by inch, then a ripening, the surprise of letting go. She imagined a lover beside her on the blanket, naked beside her in the woods. What would he be like? She looked at her body, long, slender, with the firm curved ripeness, the color of an apricot, and put another body beside it, long and slender and the same golden rosy color. She lay on her side, one arm beneath her flushed cheek, and pushed her pelvis toward the empty side of the blanket, slowly fitted the other body to hers, down to the mingling of toes, and her back would curve in as though someone were stroking it sensuously, and sometimes she would sling her free arm across space heavy with pollen and sunlight; she would sigh and close her eyes tight, and smile.

In late afternoon, when the sun passed her clearing and left it cool and shady, she walked. She put on jeans and sneakers and walked down the hill to the mailbox. Sometimes she put in a letter to Cameron. Sometimes she found one waiting for her, addressed in his flat, assured handwriting, beneath the impressive letterhead, cold to her touch from lying in the shadows of the box. He hoped her holiday was being restorative, he said. He hoped she was resting, gathering her energies for the fray. She pictured herself leaving him, packing her clothes and announcing she wanted a divorce. In this fantasy, her back was always turned to him, she was afraid to confront his face.

She no longer expected miracles from her tea hours with Kate. She took them for what they were, a sharing of vitamins and tea, an exchange of harmless, affectionate pleasantries, while more important thoughts coursed privately along inside.

"Do you hope for a boy or a girl?" she asked her mother. She thought of her lover in the woods. As yet she had not been able to give him a face. He would be young, she had decided that. She imagined him giving her a baby, planting more life on her in all that rosy sunshine. She closed her eyes, there at the table with Kate, and gave a little shudder.

"A boy," said Kate. "A boy can get along better. What's the matter?"

"Nothing. Tea going down gives such a nice delicious warmth."

One afternoon, about a week and a half before she was due to leave, Francesca was lying in the sun in her favorite position. She had perfected this daily imagining to such an art that she really felt the physical presence of this lover, he was able to stir her into a prolonged, delightful state of consciousness where she knew the exact location of every molecule of her body, and where those molecules stopped and the molecules of other substances (blanket, air, trees) began. And yet her body did not confine her. She could lie there and yet float, as light and gold as a sunbeam, above the tops of trees. She could be inside a bird, fly all the way down to Claretown to the little bus station, fly fifty miles cross country to the town where she had been a child, looking down at the tops of buildings, the boutiques on Brown Street, then up to their former mountain to the beautiful house. As a bird, she thought she spied a piece of Jonathan's wrecked helicopter, gleaming silver in the sun . . .

She opened her eyes and blinked drowsily. An image slowly formed. Stretched out parallel to her, several yards away, on a fallen tree, was a long, gleaming snake. His eyes were open, she could actually see the life in them, glittering beneath the slanted lids. His body at its thickest part was as round as her calf. Time stopped as the two creatures regarded each other. Then suddenly, a flash and a rustle, and he was gone. She was lying, frozen to her spot, staring wildly at a dead tree.

She burst into tears. Shivering, she put on her shorts and shirt and stumbled down the hill toward the house, not wanting to leave that other place, yet knowing she would never again go back. Ware had just driven up and was getting out of the Land Rover.

"My gosh, what's wrong, Francesca? What's the matter?"

She ran right into his arms. "A snake. I saw this snake," she sobbed. "He was lying right next to me. He might have been lying there for hours!"

"It's all right," he said, patting her. She was trembling. She could smell his odor, rather babyish and sweet and clean. How could Kate love him as a man? "What color was it? Did it have a design on its back?"

"I couldn't tell," she wailed. "He was black, a shiny black."

"Oh that was probably just a black snake! He was probably a good snake, the kind that keeps the poisonous ones away. Poor baby, you're really shaking. It's all right, it's over now. He was probably more scared of you than you were of him."

"No he wasn't either," she said coldly, taking herself back from Ware. He stood puzzled, his plump arms dangling at his sides, bewildered at Kate's beautiful, moody daughter. Francesca went into the house, no longer crying.

Kate sat at the table, looking fresh from her afternoon nap. "What happened?"

Francesca went to her porch room and slammed the door.

She heard them talking. ". . . *happened*?" "Francesca saw a black snake. I told her . . . was . . . harmless . . ." "Harmless or not . . . woman's nature to fear a snake . . ." came Kate's reply. The voices droned on. Francesca caught Kate's ". . . getting restless. She'll be glad to leave . . ."

That night she had a nightmare about her return to Cameron. She woke in a cold sweat. She had kicked off her blankets and her body was frozen. She fished them up and lay clutching them up to her chin. The stars in the black sky blinked impersonally down on her terror.

The next day, to expiate the dream, she wrote Cameron a chatty letter. She told the snake story and said she had been scared half to death. She also told the dream, adding how foolish the whole day had been. She avoided the woods. Walking back up the hill after mailing the letter, she felt disgusted with herself. She had misrepresented herself. The snake experience had perhaps been too deep for words, and she had obscured it forever by dismissing it so lightly.

She took sunbaths close to the house. The delicious sensuous states were gone. She wished merely to preserve her suntan, of which she'd become rather proud.

One day, when Kate was off on a walk by herself, Francesca went to their bedroom and looked around. There was a four-poster bed with an old plaid spread, a chest of drawers with a vase of zinnias on it and a Bible. The floor was bare except for a small but pretty hooked rug by the bed. Beneath the bed were several pairs of shoes, Ware's and Kate's. There was a work table and chair by the window overlooking the garden. On this table was Kate's typewriter in its powder-blue case and some sewing. Francesca went closer and saw that Kate had been making baby clothes, stitching them by hand. In this room there was no trace of fur coats, creams, or jewels.

At last it was time to leave. Both women had trouble concealing their relief that the visit was over. Only Ware seemed truly sad that Francesca would not be there when they all woke up the next morning. He said this. He said,

"But at least I feel we've given you a rest." He gave her a pamphlet on vitamins and wrote down the address of a place in New Jersey where she could order the ones she needed at a discount. He patted Kate, who had gotten out of bed very early to see her daughter off, and took Francesca's bags out to the Land Rover.

"You don't mind my not coming, do you?" said Kate. "The road is so bumpy and having a baby at my age isn't the safest thing to do."

"Of course I don't mind. You will take care of yourself, won't you?" Francesca felt a little like crying.

"We will take care of each other," said Kate.

The two women looked at each other. Neither made a move to touch. Francesca heard Ware coming back to the house.

"I'm thinking about leaving Cameron," she blurted suddenly.

Kate sighed. "I always thought he was cold. But you seemed to want it. Well, you'll do what you have to do. But remember, for some of us, having a man is nothing to sneeze at."

When the Greyhound left Claretown and the waving Ware behind, Francesca settled back and pondered these remarks of Kate's. She tried to work some message into them, but wasn't sure how. Who had she meant by *some of us*?

But as the bus gathered momentum, she stopped doubting. The swift progress of the Greyhound was an extension of her own progress. She would go back to Cameron and discuss it sensibly. There did not have to be any nasty, quick rupture. She would simply tell him how she felt. If he begged her to stay with him until his own triumph was secured . . . *this* particular triumph, not all the future ones he might be planning for himself . . . well, she would stay graciously for . . . how long? A year at the most.

No, she might weaken again, lose her energy, if she stayed a year. She would go back, be decent to him for a day or so, then tell him. Be firm. Explain to him how she had been so dead and now had come to life. How she wanted to venture forth, experiment with life, explore her limits and extensions, feel passion . . .

The bus was ahead of schedule and she had extra time after her taxi left her at the airport. She bought a fashion magazine and wandered around the terminal, fingering things in the souvenir shop, studying the time differences on a row of wall clocks labeled NEW YORK, SAN FRANCISCO, HONG KONG, ROME, LONDON . . . Cameron would just be getting up now. It gave her confidence to think of him trapped three hours away from her in his separate time zone. As she walked back and forth in the terminal, enjoying the sway of her own body, reaffirming herself in a mirror here and there, a man kept watching her. He was seated near the clocks himself, checking his watch from time to time, and looking rather pleased with the bustle around him and with the prospect of flying somewhere. She wondered where. He was very attractive, sitting there in his smart gray suit, with his attaché case beside his feet, smiling vaguely at the throng and especially at her. A young executive with so many colors in his face and hair. A firm, clear face with very dark, alert eyes, and thick brown-gold hair, sunbleached. There would be important papers in his case. He would be expected, awaited somewhere. When he walked into the room with that smile, someone would look up and think happily, "Here's ——, back at last!" He had the sort of appearance that could bring only good news.

Her flight was called. The man rose, picked up his case. Francesca bowed her head and hurried modestly ahead of him to the plane. She found a window seat, buckled herself in quickly, turned the pages of her magazine. She felt him board the plane.

"Excuse me, is this seat taken?" A nice voice, sure of itself behind its politeness.

"No, it's free."

"Good." He folded something and put it above on the rack. Sat down, placed the case beneath his seat, buckled himself in. Francesca studied the exotic poses of models diligently. Her skin felt warm, as though the sun were shining on it again.

He said nothing till they were taking off. "Are you flying far?"

"To California," she said. "And you?"

"Only to New York this evening," he said.

Francesca looked at his face. It was very close to hers, their two heads resting against the high seats. She remembered her lover of the woods and suddenly saw this man's face on him. She closed her eyes.

"Are you all right?"

"Oh yes." She opened her eyes. His face seemed closer.

"I thought you were fainting."

"No, I was thinking."

He laughed. "It must have been some thought."

"It was," she said, blushing.

They continued to look at each other, faces almost touching, while their bodies remained securely fastened in upright positions.

7 CAMERON AWAITS FRANCESCA

Cameron woke early on Sunday, which annoyed him, as he had planned to sleep late. Francesca's delinquency had cut a hole in his schedule and he had to fill it in. This morning, which was to have been reunion morning (he had planned a breakfast of popovers, *omelette fines herbes*, and a blueberry and mango compote he had invented himself), he was spending alone in bed. Last night, after his second nine holes, which he played badly, he had eaten in a Chinese restaurant in town, where he was known. Then he had walked and thought. He paid a visit to Crystal Gardens, that outdoor residence of the degenerate young, the source of so many headaches for the city. A philanthropist who had been bitten by the youth-and-relevance bug in his eighties had given a fifteen-acre walled garden adjoining his estate to the city on the condition that no young person who needed a place to sleep would ever be evicted. The city said they didn't want it under such conditions. Cameron said, take it. But every hippie and drug addict in town will use it as a crashing pad, they protested. Take it, Cameron said. Let them come. We'll know where they are. But the filth, the sanitation problems. So, put in a couple of toilets. Maybe even a shower under the trees. Build them a lovely outdoor prison. They'll maintain it. Cameron, do you really think . . .? Sure. I think of all the hours it will save our boys . . .

Now Cameron often went and sat in this rapidly deteriorating walled garden which had been christened Crystal Gardens by the narcs who languidly conducted their periodic raids, making thirty or forty arrests every time. Still, the place filled with newcomers. They mingled with the longer-term residents, building little communal campfires which scorched the grass, making welfare babies at night under the trees, strumming and living their dream. It calmed Cameron to come here, dressed in his elegant clothes, and sit in full view of them on a wooden bench under a eucalyptus tree. The politics of it interested him. They liked him in a way. He would stroll a while first, before sitting down, nodding to familiar faces along the way. Some of them nodded back. He often wondered how he came across to them, what archetype he played in their drug-induced dramas. He had some pretty good ideas. Last night, a girl who had just been released from prison again waved her baby's hand at Cameron as he ambled by with his odd duck walk. She looked really glad to see him again. She knew, many of them knew, that Cameron was the one who was responsible for their indefinite lease in the Garden. He was their landlord in a sense.

Cameron reached out and took a letter from the bedside table. He had already read it many times. It was Francesca's last letter written from Kate's. After informing him of her flight times back, which he already had written carefully in his memo book, she related a nightmare she'd had about him.

"We'd just come back from the airport and you said to go up in the elevator while you parked the car. Our apartment was draped in sheets. There was an operating table set up. A surgeon with a black mask said, 'Get undressed, Francesca, we haven't much time.' There was an arrogant nurse, also in black, with big breasts, and she said to me, 'Here, quick, slip into this.' (An operating gown.) I ran out of the apartment back to the elevator just as it opened and you got out, also wearing a black mask . . ."

"I'm such a villain," murmured Cameron. He replaced the letter in its envelope. "I want her to be happy and therefore I am such a villain."

He got up and made himself breakfast, interrupted once by his secretary, who was working overtime and couldn't find something, and once by someone calling to remind him of an eight a.m. emergency session of the Crime Commission tomorrow morning, Monday morning. Son of a bitch. That meant there could be no time for the special

welcome-home breakfast of popovers, omelet, and compote. Cameron was disappointed. Such ceremonies were
important to him.

He sat eating his breakfast, sipping the freshly ground
coffee, wiping his lips with a napkin, thinking. He was not
a villain, no. Unless your definition of a villain was that of
a person who spent his whole life being disappointed in
people. Whose fault was it if people entered his life dis-
guised as more than they were and, once inside, flung off
their masks with relief and revealed their paltry selves?
They then blamed him for not approving of them any
more. They called him "inhuman," "unable to love," "sadis-
tic." By human they usually meant mixed up, a mess of
unthought-out reactions. By love they usually meant need
or fear. And his sadism was simply a matter of letting
them stew in their own juice while he looked on, arms
folded over his chest, a curious wonderment in his eyes
that they could not see, could not really see, that they
had jumped into their dreary mess all by themselves.

Your standards are too rigid, Cameron, acquaintances
had said to him for years.

But I don't ask anything of anyone that I wouldn't ask
of myself twice over, he would reply, meaning it. He knew
he had more will, more energy, more patience to wait for
what he wanted, more intelligence than most people. The
majority of people did not know what they wanted. They
had vague feelings, but could not sit down and write out a
list of what they wanted, what was good for them.
Cameron knew what he wanted, what was good for him;
he carried a neat list in his head, arranged in priorities. He

also knew what was good for others. Now the time was coming when his milieu recognized this. He was ready. He had the energy to spare. He had not changed through the years; it was the times that had changed. He stayed the same, a fixed point, and waited for the times to return to him.

As he was washing the dishes, the telephone rang. He plucked at the rubber gloves, but they stuck to his hands. He grabbed a dishcloth and dried off his gloved hands and picked up the receiver in the bedroom.

"Cameron? Where were you?" Francesca's voice, crackling over the wire, guilty.

Cameron looked at his watch. "I was in the kitchen. I hope *you* are at the airport."

"Actually . . . I'm not."

"I see." He waited.

"Cameron? Would you mind if I stayed on in the city for another week? I thought . . . well, I thought I might shop for some clothes. Some of the new fashions are really fabulous, I've been looking at the new magazines alone in my room."

I wonder who he is, thought Cameron, massaging the yellow rubber fingers against one another.

"Cameron? Are you still there?"

"I'm here, Francesca. But what about money? You'll need money if you're going to shop."

"Oh money! Well I have all of my traveler's checks. There was certainly nothing to spend them on at Kate's. I have my credit cards."

"You won't buy many fabulous clothes for the amount

of those checks, love. And the good stores won't take your cards." He knew he was making her squirm a little. "What I'll do is this: are you listening?"

"Yes," she said. Meekly.

"Tomorrow morning, first thing, I'll wire a bank draft to First National City Bank, the one at Park and Fifty-third. It will be made out in your name. You won't be able to shop before early afternoon, because of our time lag, will that inconvenience you too much?"

"Oh no, oh no! Not at all. Oh Cameron—"

"Will a week be long enough, Francesca?"

"Oh yes, I mean—Cameron, you aren't mad?"

"Why on earth should I be? I'm disappointed, of course. I have missed you. But you are your own woman and I want to help you preserve that status. I will ask two things—"

"Oh, sure. What?"

"Both for my own peace of mind. One is that you stay in a decent hotel. The other is that you promise to give me a call, sometime during the week, some promised time that I can look forward to. Let's say . . ." He thought carefully. "Thursday night."

"That's a promise. Both things." Oh she was relieved. Relieved and guilty.

"Now I must go and see what I can do about salvaging my poor Sunday," he said.

"Oh, Cameron—"

"Till Thursday, my love."

He returned to the kitchen and finished washing the dishes. He dried them. Then he sponge-mopped the floor.

He stood at the edge of the room, arms hugged tight against his chest, watching the water dry in little patches. He got out the container of liquid wax and some clean cloths and worked himself scrupulously around the floor on all fours till he saw a reflection of his bland, impassive face upon his handiwork. He glanced at his watch. Not even noon! He stood up, feeling a little displaced, and wandered into the bedroom, going again to her closet. Once again he stood in its enclosure. He breathed her perfume, a perfume which he had selected for her himself, a costly, haunting scent. How he wished he could break every other bottle of this perfume in the world, so that this scent would be identified as his wife's alone! He touched her dresses, her shoes, which she always kicked off, left anywhere, and he himself replaced on the rack. Here was that white Roman toga he had bought her, she had never worn it, it was after she had stopped going to parties. She had tried it on only once, in this room. Now the fact that he alone had seen Francesca in this garment was in its favor. With a rapt expression on his face, he removed it from the garment bag. He carried its softness to the bed and sat down with it draped across his lap, musing over it.

Then, with a deep sigh, he lay back on the bed and covered himself with the garment. He breathed the scent of her perfume.

8 THE LOVER

"I don't want to go back to Cameron, Mike."

"No reason why you should."

"But what could I do instead?"

"Any number of things. What would you have done if you had never met him?"

"I don't know. I had no idea what I was going to do when I did meet him. In a way he saved me from having to find out."

"Well, now you can find out."

Mike's voice sounded cheerful. She lay in the hollow of his shoulder and would not look at his face. She had planned this dialogue since early this morning, Sunday, and it was a very important juncture. Therefore she didn't have the courage to look at his face, she couldn't risk seeing the slightest sign on it that he was indifferent to her. He was the tenderest, most thoughtful lover she had ever known, but he was maddeningly impersonal in conversation. He evaded every attempt on her part to make him talk about himself. They had spent almost twenty-four hours in this room together, having their meals sent up, and she knew no more about him—except that he called himself Mike—than she had when they met on the plane. What he did for a living, whether or not he was married, where he came from, where he was flying off to, none of this had he volunteered. Francesca felt her well-being eroding as she contemplated his Monday morning takeoff. The well-being was replaced with a determination to find out where she stood with him and to get some commitment out of him. She was beginning to see this was not going to be easy.

"You know what I wish," she said, attempting lightness, "I wish we could stay here forever in this lovely, bright room, with all the jets crossing over us and leaving us behind. Just calling down to room service whenever we felt hungry."

She waited.

He lit a cigarette, keeping her balanced on his chest. She swiveled her eye up just in time to see him exhale. His face was calm, pleasant, but unreadable.

"You'd soon grow tired of that," he said at last.

"You mean you would."

"We both would."

Francesca lay very still. She felt frozen.

He stroked her hair. "It has been beautiful," he said. "Beautiful. But we both have things to do."

"What do you have to do?"

"I'm a working man, Francesca."

"What kind of work? What kind of work do you do?"

"Well, I'm a salesman."

"I don't believe you. You don't look like a salesman, you don't dress like one. You don't act like one. You're too distant ever to sell anything."

"Okay," he said cheerfully. He continued to smoke. She resented his relationship with the cigarette, it put that much more space between them.

"What do *I* have to do?" she said. "Please tell me that."

"You must discover it."

"And where am I going to do that?" she asked, a little angry.

He laughed. "Where are you going to discover it? If I could tell you, then it wouldn't be a discovery. You'd simply be following my directions."

"Oh—!" Francesca turned away from him. She drew herself up in a ball and ground her eyelids tight together. A tear squeezed out. She wished she would flood the room in tears and wash them both away in the torrent of her need. She did not want it to be over with this man. She did not want to go back to Cameron. In between yawned a terrible blank gulf which Mike seemed to be trying to push her into.

"Come back, Francesca. It's lonely without you." She

heard him put out his cigarette in the ashtray. He slid over to her and curled his body to the back of her, burrowed his face into her hair. She felt him grow hard. This both annoyed her and gave her a sense of power.

"Mike, will we see each other again?"

"I hope so. Do you? If you stay in the city we will. I get down here pretty regularly . . ."

Down from where?

". . . but I wouldn't want you to stay here just because of me. I would want it to be for yourself, for your discovery that we were talking about."

"It wouldn't be just for you," she put in. She was becoming hopeful again.

"That makes me feel much better." He snuggled closer, his body hinting, urging her to turn over. But she was not ready yet.

"Do you think I could get a job, Mike?"

"Sure you could."

"How does a person go about getting a job?"

He sighed. She felt him shift moods a little, then lapse back into his desire for her. "I'll tell you what," he said softly against the back of her ear. "I'll inaugurate you, I'll get you started. We'll check out of here this afternoon and I'll ride into the city with you and we'll find you a hotel, something decent but inexpensive so you can stay away from that bank draft at First National, and I'll take a room for the night in this same hotel and then we'll go out and have dinner and get an early edition of tomorrow's newspaper and we'll go through the want ads together. We'll get you all set up for your emancipation."

Something was bothering her. "But the other money I

have . . . the traveler's checks, the credit cards even . . . Cameron gave me those as well. He'll still be financing my emancipation."

"Not really," her lover said impatiently, "not really. When you accepted that money, you accepted it in good faith as his wife. You had no plans for leaving him. As long as you take nothing from him after you decide you no longer wish to be his wife, your emancipation slate is clean."

"You are a salesman, after all, aren't you, Mike?"

"I have something else I'd like to sell you."

"Oh what?"

"Turn over and I'll show you."

9 INTO THE CITY

After a long, hot taxi ride from the airport, Mike checked them into a modest hotel in the west fifties. He seemed to have a past acquaintance with it, but when Francesca asked him if he'd stayed here before he looked surprised and said no. He arranged for her to have a room with shared bath on the third floor for the weekly rate of fifty-two dollars. He took a double room on the seventeenth floor for himself, which cost twenty-one dollars for overnight. A gnomelike black man whose uniform smelled musty took their bags and led the way to the elevators. The elevator on the right had a sign posted on its doors, OUT OF ORDER, so the three of them had to wait until the working elevator descended from the twenty-fifth floor.

"Shall we stop and see your room first, get you settled in?" he asked.

"No, let's just go straight to your room," Francesca said.

"Whatever you say." He ruffled her hair as they got into the elevator with the bellman. "But you have to see your room sometime, you know."

"I know," she replied glumly. The palms of her hands grew cold as she contemplated that moment. They rode the seventeen floors in silence. Francesca thought Mike had changed since they had left their airport hide-away. He was more distracted, businesslike. He frowned up at the numbers above the bald head of the bellman. His face seemed to have changed color and texture: there was a formal gray cast to it and the skin looked rough, rather like pavement. They reached seventeen. Francesca followed the two men down a dim hallway, feeling forgotten. There was an old smell about this hotel, of long-worn carpets and radiator pipes. Thick brown doors poked their convex surfaces out into the hall. The black gnome unlocked a door and entered the room, going straight to the air-conditioner and turning a dial. A clattering, metallic whir started up. Frowning, Mike paid the man. The heavy brown door swung shut and they were alone together.

Francesca sat down on the side of the double bed, which seemed a cot compared to the cerise-covered king-sized one at their airport hideaway. She was sorry they had left that other bright room, with the birds and the jets, and wondered if Mike was blaming her. "This is not exactly the luxury suite," she tried to joke.

"Are you kidding? This is the best room in the house." He unzipped his suitcase, removed his shaving kit, and zipped up the big case again. In the other place, he had taken out his suits and hung them in the closet, spread himself out. Now he was rationing himself, not committing himself to this room he must leave so early tomorrow morning, almost two hours earlier than if he had stayed at the airport motel. Did he hold this against her? Was he regretting his offer to launch her in her independence? She was afraid to ask. She felt like an intruder in this room. Also, she needed to go to the bathroom, but didn't dare ask him to get out. He was in there, the door open, arranging items from his shaving kit. She could hear various clinks on the porcelain basin. What she should have done, what would have been more graceful, was to have left him at her own floor, settled herself into *her* territory —her launching pad—and freshened up in privacy.

She could still do this, get up, collect her lightweight suitcase, and say casually, "I have a few things I want to do. I'll meet you in the lobby in half an hour." Going away from him, even for a little while, would make him cherish her again. She would go down and use her bathroom in peace and splash water on her face and brush her hair till it shone. He would be struck anew by her.

She stood up, ready to speak. Could he hear her over the air-conditioner? She waited till he came out of the bathroom, having splashed water on *his* face, smiling and pleased with himself. "You know what I think we should do now?" he said jauntily, "go out for a walk, look around the city. Work up an appetite."

Agreeing, she asked if she could just use his bathroom first. Inside, she ran both faucets and tried to aim for the side of the bowl. At the other place, newer and modern, there had not been the problem. The rooms were spacious, set far apart. Also the water level in the other toilet was lower. Suddenly she remembered Cameron's faucet fetish and for the first time saw his side and felt sorry for him. It must be a terrible burden, preserving your perfect image for a loved one around the clock.

Out on the street, things got better. It was a hot August Sunday, but clear, and with a breeze from the river. Francesca liked walking beside Mike, making a couple. Most of the other people walking were in couples. Many had dogs, well-kept, elegant dogs; well-kept, foolish little dogs, on leashes. Francesca looked at herself walking beside this graceful, serious man, in the plate glass of the windows they passed. She imagined herself married to him and even went so far as to imagine the dog they would have. She decided on a silver afghan and was so carried away by the image that she smiled up at him and squeezed his hand. Another couple, not so handsome, turned to stare enviously. Mike noticed this and smiled, the first time since he'd come into the city. He put his arm around her shoulder and guided her up and down various streets and avenues, pointing out sights, examples of good architecture, bad architecture. Perhaps he was an architect, she thought, noticing nothing except whether they were in step or not, how often he smiled.

She made him smile again when, ordering dinner in a Greek restaurant, she confessed to him that she knew nothing about Greek food. This was a lie, she and Kate had spent part of a spring in Greece. But he patted her hand and told her to sit back and drink her cocktail, "I know just what you'll love." She had seen her favorite dish on the menu, an eggplant and lamb combination, and hoped he would order that. He ordered shish kebab for both, and she thought *it serves me right* and wished she were going to have a bedside chat later with the old Kate on this matter of making men smile.

They ate and drank too much and returned to the hotel and made love. Francesca kept slipping off into feverish reveries in which too many images left over from the day seemed crowded inside her eyelids. At other times, she fought off a vague feeling of nausea. And then suddenly the lovemaking was over and Mike was asleep. She lay beside him and her mind perversely wakened until everything appeared painfully sharp and clear.

The luminous hands on his wristwatch indicated half past eleven. Only half past eleven, and they had planned to stay up most of the night, talking and looking through the want ads for possible jobs. But the paper lay on the glass-topped dressing table, along with the room key, the necktie, her purse. And now it was over, she had been scarcely conscious of any of it, and in less than six hours he would wake and shave and go forever from this room. She felt cheated! There he lay, so peacefully, snoring just a little. He slept on his back, one arm resting behind his head, bent at the elbow. She could just make out the lines of his profile, a dark jagged line: mountainous borders of a country closed to her.

"Mike?" she whispered softly. If only he would wake and they could finish the evening as planned. "Mike?" He slept on.

Suddenly she wanted to penetrate that country. She was terrified at what she wanted to do. Heart pounding, she eased off the mattress and padded across to the dressing table. It was too dark to see anything, so she groped along surfaces with the flat of her hand: not here. Where did men keep their wallets, where did Cameron keep his? Funny, she couldn't remember. Pants, coat? Where were his pants? She found her own dress and a bra flung over the chair. She felt her way to the closet. The door squeaked! If only they hadn't felt cold and turned the air-conditioner down to low. She could use all the added clatter she could get. She stopped and listened, standing just inside the closet door. He had stopped snoring, but was breathing deeply, evenly. She felt for the pants. They hung, neatly creased, on the hanger. Even in the midst of all that passion, he had found time to hang up the pants he would wear on the plane tomorrow morning. She felt inside the coat. Ah, there it was. Shaking, she drew it out. It was thick, filled with stuff. She had all the things he wouldn't tell her between these five fingers. Now a light. She must find light. Why not simply take the wallet, lock herself into the bathroom and go through everything brazenly, at leisure. Even if he woke, he would not think anything of hearing her in the bathroom. She could sit there at her leisure and shuffle through the story of his life like cards, learn his age, his weight, his occupation, his credit rating, his military service record, his indulgences; she might find illustrations as well: a younger Mike, a military Mike, Mike's woman, Mike's women . . . *Mike's wife and children . . .*

But she knew she was too fainthearted to make it to the bathroom. Instead she fumbled on through other pockets till she found what she wanted, a book of matches. Then, pulling the closet door closed behind her (it squeaked again!) she lit a match and flipped open the wallet. Some kind of ID. A green background. Facts and figures jumped before her eyes, she must focus on one. Birth date, January something, 1937 . . . Michael S. . . . what? . . . Rushing, Reusing?

The match went out. Shaking and sweating, the closet was very hot, she lit another. Perhaps she should go through quickly, look for pictures, *the* picture, that woman's face, perhaps flanked by young faces, the evidence she dreaded. She began pulling stuff out. It was packed in so tightly, perhaps years of evidence in here, layers and layers of Mike, of Michael S. Reusing, Rushing, or had she only imagined she saw Rushing because she was rushing so, to keep from being discovered in her crime?

She dropped the match on the coat. There was a nasty burning smell and sparks. The match fell to the floor and went out. The cards came flying from the wallet like impatient birds released from a cage.

"Francesca?"

She bolted from the closet, managing to bang the bathroom door in passing.

"Yes?" She slid weakly in beside him.

"What-dnuh . . . noise?" He had shifted to his left side. His back was to her.

"I just went to the bathroom."

"Uhhh." Soon he was snoring again. She lay, unable to move, the arm beneath her falling asleep, staring at the faint white curve of his back.

After a time, she got up the courage to slide from the mattress, crawl along the floor to the closet, feel around the dusty, gritty floor until every card had been collected and replaced. Of course he would find her out, but she prayed for it to be after he had left the hotel. She could never manage to put the cards back in order. Well, since you've been caught, why not light one more match and have a last look-through, came a flat, wry voice from the depths of her frustration. But she could not manage one more feat after the very considerable one of standing up inside the closet and finally relocating the inside jacket pocket and filling it with the wallet.

When his desk call came, she pretended to be asleep. He got up at once and went into the bathroom, leaving the door ajar. Water splashed, the clink of jars and bottles. She heard him lathering his face. The room was filling with an ugly gray daylight, seeping in between the cracks in the blinds. Opening one eye, she discovered she could see a part of his face as reflected in the bathroom mirror through the half-open door. It was an awful sight, like two sides of a dead white triangle, a mask with slits for eyes and a grim, pink mouth. A disembodied hand, also reflected, appeared and began to slice away the face in even strokes.

She kept her eyes closed while he dressed, shamming

deep breathing when he went to his closet and took down his pants, tugged his coat from the hanger. She waited for him to curse when he discovered the burn. Had it left a big hole? Could it be possible that it had not left anything at all?

He sat down on the bed. He smelled all fresh and presentable to the public, all trace of her had been scoured away with the hotel soap. "Francesca?"

She opened her eyes. There was the old Mike, the Mike of the airport era, those perfect hours before the city, smiling down at her! With a hand still cold from all that washing, he stroked her hair away from her warm forehead. "Aren't you going to tell me goodbye? I'm off. Are you going to be okay? Will you go through with it? I'm sorry about falling asleep, we drank too quickly before the food came."

"It's all right."

"Look, I was thinking while I was shaving. I think you should go to a good employment agency. They charge a fee, your first week's salary usually, but they smooth things for you. They give you names of places that need people and you are sent to those places. You are expected. I think that might be better. It will give you security."

"Will I ever see you again, Mike?"

He rumpled her hair. "If you stay in this city, I'll tell you one thing: you'll have to run pretty fast to keep from seeing me. I'll keep in touch, Francesca. In fact, how about this, I'll give you a call Thursday night, about eight, just to check on you, see that you haven't found someone else . . ."

"Oh how can you say that!"

"And if you haven't," he went on, enjoying his little joke, "who knows? I might even arrange it so I can get back for the weekend. Would you be free if I could arrange it, Francesca?"

"Oh. Yes. I'd be free."

He bent down and kissed her while she was still shyly fumbling with her surprise, and just as the passion which had cheated her last night began to make its delinquent return he left her, neatly, quickly. The room was emptied of him as though he had never been. She ran to the bathroom to reassure herself. He must have left some trace. The small bar of soap was still wet. She picked it up and smelled it. It was all she had of him. The mirror which had so recently contained his image was empty now. It held only her face.

10   CONTAINERS

"Cameron? Nathan here. I hate to disturb you and Francesca on Sunday."

"You didn't. Francesca is in New York. I persuaded her to stay over and buy some clothes."

"Wonderful. You prepare for everything, don't you? Look, I've set up the dinner for next week, okay? A week from this coming Wednesday. She'll be back by then, won't she?"

"She'll be back at the end of the week."

"Fine, fine. Things are starting to pop. Did you see Bernice's column? There was a mention of Francesca. Bernice compared her to a medieval virgin."

"I liked that, yes. I've saved the column for Francesca."

"I'm afraid you're being cast as the Grand Inquisitor, my boy. But that's okay too."

"Yes, I think so. People are ready for a change."

Nathan laughed. "I've got the dinner set up. Formal dress, formal everything, as you specified. It will be a period piece, I've got the caterers working on it. That's a week from Wednesday. If you could get together a few remarks, your ideas and ideals—"

"My ideas and ideals are already together, Nathan."

"I know. I know they are. Well, I'll get busy on things. I'll call you again tomorrow. Meanwhile, if you want me, you know where to find me."

"Thank you, Nathan." The two men hung up.

Cameron went out for a walk. He was generating too much energy, he had to move fast in order to contain it. It was early afternoon. He covered miles of the city, his long shadow skimming through the constituencies. At last he achieved a pace wherein his inner rhythms so clarified they seemed to displace the weight of his body. At such times, Cameron felt as though he were flying. He was his thoughts in flight.

In mid-flight, he collided with a Negro child who was chasing a basketball toward the street. The impact of the two bodies knocked the child down and sent Cameron reeling against a wall, banging his shoulderbone. At that moment a speeding pizza delivery truck burst the ball beneath its wheels. The child began to shriek.

"Stop that," said Cameron, setting him back on his feet. He held the boy's shoulders and gazed into his eyes. "Would you rather be squashed yourself? Learn to look ahead. You may not have the luck to bump into me next time." The boy, looking terrified, wrenched away from Cameron and shot off down an alley.

Meanwhile, the driver of the truck had screeched to a stop, double parked, jumped out, and retrieved the flattened ball. A young man with floppy blond hair, he approached Cameron sheepishly, holding the smashed object in front of him, this evidence of his crime.

"Where'd the kid go? I feel awful about this. I'll buy him another ball."

"He's gone," said Cameron, massaging his own shoulder. He looked the young man over curiously. "Why should you buy him another ball? It was equally his foolishness. You shouldn't have been speeding, but neither should his ball have been in the street. You are compounding the disorder now, however, by double parking."

The young driver gaped at Cameron. "What kind of a nut are you? Jesus Christ!" He ran off, down the alley, after the child.

"Not that nut, no," murmured Cameron. He resumed his walk, noting the license number of the double-parked pizza truck.

Back at the apartment, he went at once to his study and opened a drawer in his desk. Up rose a tape recorder. Cameron put a new tape on the spools, pushed a button, and leaned back in his chair. He made a steeple with the tips of his long, skinny fingers and, for several moments, meditated against the soft swish of the waiting tape.

"Shortly after I learned that I would have the honor of addressing you tonight, I went out for one of my customary walks through the city. I walked and I thought—it was, as you know, a beautiful afternoon, the sort of airy, untroubled afternoon which tempts one to think that all those stories of violence and pollution are fictions constructed by a reader-hungry press. (But of course, alas, they are not fictions. Not *all* of them, at any rate.)

"As I walked through the various neighborhoods, I was thinking: what could I say to you this evening? What shape could I give to my thoughts so that you might hold them, as solidly and as clearly, as I myself do?

"Suddenly a child dashed in front of me. He was chasing his basketball into the busy street. He was after that ball and thinking of nothing else. A truck was speeding past, and, well, the conjunction would have been tragic indeed had I not been there to reach out and grab that impetuous little soul.

"I walked on, a little shaken, thinking of the incident. I was also thinking of my wife, who is here beside me tonight. I had persuaded her to stay over in New York and do some shopping. As I walked, I imagined her moving alone, somewhere in that other city, alone and free, her own woman, yet secure in the knowledge that I was here, imagining her.

"And suddenly I saw the shape which would convey to you the way I feel about the things which concern us all.

"You see I believe in shapes. I believe everything good

has a shape. Shapes are the way in which we know who we are and where we are in our universe. Show me the shapes and forms a man gives to his life, and I will tell you whether he is master or victim of that life. Someone once asked Confucius: 'If you were king, what is the first thing you would do?' 'I would give everything in the kingdom a name,' he said. If I were Attorney General, I would give everything a shape.

"The shape I saw as I walked, the shape I want to share with you because it best expresses our mutual concerns, is that of a container. Like this brandy snifter. Containers. Relationships are containers. Marriages are containers. Friendships and families are containers. They provide a finite form in which we can store our identities; they are safe-deposit boxes, shared with another, with others, for our personal histories.

"Our state government is also such a container.

"In a marriage, a traditional marriage let us say, the husband is the public container. He gives his wife his name, his social and financial backing, he insulates her from certain outside infringements in order that she may have the leisure and security to develop her inner life, to blossom forth as a container for their private life.

"In friendships, the same. Though there are many patterns, of course. A Martha to a Mary. A patron to a poet. There are many, many combinations of container and contained. But the requisites are always the same. Each provides the other with a refuge in time of trouble, with a continuum to fall back on in time of self-doubt, with an underpinning of earned trust upon which it is possible to build new achievements.

"A good government does likewise. Provides the refuge, the protection, the continuum, the underpinning. Certain men are the husbands, the Marthas, the patrons. They offer their energies as a sort of cordon to contain the desires and abilities of those inside. They agree to become containers so that the contained can go about their business, their art, their invention, their meditation, whatever they have elected themselves to do for the enrichment of the total shape.

"Of course there are good and bad containers. A container should not be too thick, too rigid. Then the glass becomes cloudy, it becomes opaque to the needs of both sides, a blind prison wall. It is no longer capable of ringing. The brandy loses its aroma.

"But it can't be too thin, too flaccid, either. In that case, what is contained spills out into license, anarchy, chaos. Boundary lines are violated. The child who only wanted to play is smashed beneath the wheels of a truck.

"Yeats, that great poet of man's politics, wrote: 'The wrong of unshapely things is a wrong too great to be told.' I believe evil is shapeless, gentlemen, and that's why it's so hard to control. It's like a spreading stain, like cells gone wild; it won't be still long enough for you to isolate it, contain its shape. I detest, therefore, all manifestations of shapelessness: meaninglessness, waste, destruction, vagueness, indecisiveness, superfluousness. I passionately abhor words and gestures which cannot contain what they mean. I confess to being an old-fashioned idealist and I'd like to propose a return to ideals. A return to meaningful shapes. May we drink to that?"

Cameron switched off the tape. He took Francesca's

photograph in its simple thin gold frame from his desk and placed it in the living room on the bare mantlepiece. For some time he stood beside it, arrested by so much perfection within a square of non-glare glass. Then he yielded to the impulse to hold the picture against his shoulder and admire the two of them in the oval mirror above the mantle: the medieval virgin and her skinny horseman, proud faces set upon the task ahead. Cleaning up after the flaccid Apocalypse.

He went back to the study and rewound the tape, pushed PLAY.

"Shortly after I learned that I would have the honor of addressing you tonight, I went out for one of my customary walks through the city," began the slow, conversational voice.

"I walked and I thought—it was, as you know, a beautiful afternoon, the sort of airy, untroubled afternoon which tempts one to think . . ."

Cameron frowned. He stopped the machine. He worked the passage over carefully, then struck the other from the tape, replaced it with the new one. He listened to the whole thing again.

Everything was going fine. He had a week and three days to get it perfect.

11   AN INTERVIEW

Light-green carpeted hall. Closed walnut doors on either side. Last one on the right. Black plaque with white letters: NINA BRETT. Francesca knocked. A nice name, Nina Brett.

"Come in. Please sit down. I'll take that," said Nina Brett.

Francesca looked at the young woman who was scanning her application. Probably no more than her own age. Formidably groomed. Her black hair looped forward in liquid-like waves, down from a dead-straight center part, decorously covered her earlobes, then coiled its shining thickness in a tight knot at the base of her skull. Her hollow-cheeked pale face was powdered paler and her narrow mouth was painted with bright red lipstick. Her dress, light gray, close-fitting, looked like a Paris designer's rendition of a prison matron's uniform. The single ornament she wore, a square-cut garnet ring, flashed occasionally under the fluorescent lights, which were beginning to give Francesca a headache. She had not eaten breakfast. She felt frowsy. She wondered if Nina Brett was married. Engaged?

"Roper College," said Nina Brett with a slight British accent. "Where is that?"

Francesca told her.

Nina blinked, obviously did not think the information worth comment, and balanced Francesca's application on the cushion of her palm, as though testing its weight.

"You've checked the box marked *separated*. Are you legally separated from Mr. Bolt?"

"Not yet," said Francesca. She leaned forward, sliding one of her elbows onto Nina's immaculate desk. "I only decided, you see, this weekend." She smiled confidentially at the other woman.

"Decided what?" asked Nina Brett, not smiling.

"To leave. To separate from Cam—from my husband."

"You are quite sure about it?"

Francesca looked straight into the cold blue eyes and repeated, "Quite sure." The judicial solemnity of that chalk face made her feel she had sworn an oath.

Nina Brett held Francesca's application firmly between both hands. For a moment Francesca wondered if she was going to tear it up. "*What* . . ." she began shrilly, then modulated her voice and began again, "What sort of employment did you have in mind? It says here you have had no previous experience."

"No previous experience," murmured Francesca humbly. She took her elbow off Nina's desk.

"How many words do you type?"

"I never learned to type. I got a B.A. in Liberal Arts. That's not good for much, is it?"

"No," said Nina Brett.

"Perhaps I could—" Francesca hesitated, not sure her idea would be well received.

"Yes?" The cold blue eyes fastened on her.

"Well, I really wouldn't mind having a job like the one you've got. Where I would sit behind a desk and talk to people."

Nina Brett's laugh was like tiny ice cubes falling into a thin glass from a great height. "I should think you wouldn't mind. Come back with a Master's Degree in Industrial Psychology and five years' experience and we'll put you on the waiting list."

"Oh," said Francesca. "I'm sorry. Well, maybe I—"

Nina's telephone rang. "Excuse me," she said. "Hello? Oh God. That devil." She glanced at the electric wall clock which said half past ten. "Looks like I'll have to. Would you mind talking to him till I come? It will take me fifteen minutes. Thank you so much." She hung up, opened her desk drawer, took out a shiny patent leather purse, and stood up.

"I'm sorry but I have to go home," she told Francesca. "My cat has got himself stuck between apartments again. That was the cleaning lady. I have to extricate him."

"Between apartments?" repeated Francesca, wanting to be sympathetic.

"Yes, I live in this—oh, there really isn't time to go into the details of this city's execrable architecture. Look, I'd transfer you over to Mr. Norberry, he's our other consultant, but the truth is there aren't any jobs for which you would qualify. Not today, anyway. Why not give me a call first thing tomorrow if you haven't come up with anything? Meanwhile, you *might* try a modeling agency. Look in the yellow pages. There are dozens of them. You may have to take off twenty pounds first."

"Twenty pounds!"

For the first time Nina Brett smiled at Francesca. She had small teeth, very white. "Yes, at least. Ten years ago you might have squeaked by as you are. Now it's the six-foot hoyden, emaciated elegance. You know. It might help if you were black. Good luck, Mrs. Bolt."

"Shall I call you tomorrow morning?" Francesca followed her to the door.

"Yes, do," said Nina Brett, and swept around the corner to the elevator.

Francesca retrieved her own purse from the floor beside Nina's desk. She wandered down the hall. A young man with reddish sideburns suddenly came out of another office. He carried a stack of folders.

"May I help you find someone?" he inquired politely. She wondered if this was Mr. Norberry, the other consultant.

"I'm just looking for the LADIES, actually," Francesca said.

"Ah. Straight ahead to the end of the hall, last door."

"Thank you."

She was relieved to find herself alone in the restroom. She went at once to the mirror. Was she fat? Had she slowly put on weight during those afternoons of idle dozing in California? Had Ware's health potions ruined her chances for emaciated elegance?

The mirror gave back the same reflection she was used to. For the first time, it seemed insufficient. For one thing, the hair . . . what a mess! She set down her purse on the shelf above the basin and rummaged around inside for a brush. She smoothed back her hair, pulled it tight against her scalp till it hurt. Oh if only she had a rubber band, some pins, something, she would make herself a knot above reproach, like Nina Brett. But for now she must be content with a good brushing. Also her skin seemed suddenly too colorful, like some common dairymaid, beside the pallor of Nina. *Come back with a Master's Degree in Industrial Psychology.* Why hadn't she worn stockings to this interview? Her bare legs looked obscene, there were hairs, even, when was the last time she had remembered to shave her legs? Not since her plucking days, over a month ago! No wonder Nina Brett had not been overjoyed about helping her. She would not dare approach a modeling agency, looking like this.

At last, after much hair-brushing and sucking in of stomach and because she knew she had to come out sometime, Francesca slunk down the hall and out of the suite of offices of the employment agency she had earlier entered so full of confidence.

She spent the morning wandering up and down the streets, in a kind of stupor, occasionally checking herself in the windows to see if she had gotten ugly, to see if she was still there. She had a weird sense of *déjà vu* about this morning. Why was that? She knew she should go back to her tiny hotel room in the west fifties, take a deep breath, sit down with the newspaper and make a note of other employment agencies. That was not the only one, Nina Brett's. Francesca had chosen it because it stood out more than some of the others, had a double line around the box. With her qualifications, or lack of them, rather, perhaps she should stay clear of the attractive ads.

She knew she would not go back to that room.

Like other solitaries who have an empty day ahead, she paced herself. She would take a lunch break at twelve, perhaps a quarter to twelve. She would think of afternoon later. Sufficient unto the morning the evils thereof.

At eleven thirty, she sat down at the counter in Schrafft's. It was beginning to fill up with women, young women like herself, only with a difference. They were settled into their lives in this city, with jobs, and friends and perhaps a cat like Nina Brett's. She ordered a tomato stuffed with tuna and a large iced tea and hoped she could make it last for an hour. While she was waiting, she fantasized about Nina Brett. What was her life like? She probably had an elegant apartment, neat and austere as her office, as her own person. *And a cleaning lady.* She pictured Nina, after work, reclining on a sofa, wearing purple silk hostess pajamas and stroking her cat. He would be Persian or Siamese (probably fixed) and have a name like Bill or Alexander. Who would the purple silk hostess pajamas be for? Francesca, now imaginatively transposed in Nina's apartment, heard the bell ring. Brittle little chimes, like Nina's laugh. Nina removed Bill/Alexander from her lap and slipped her long, pale feet into silver mules. From the back, her knot was blacker and neater than ever. She went slowly across her room and opened the door. A man stood in shadow. "Come in," said Nina Brett. He came in. "Please sit down," said Nina. He sat down on the sofa. Bill/Alexander arched his tail but did not move off. Obviously this man was not a stranger here. Now he was turning his face to Nina as he slipped off his jacket. "I'll take that," said Nina. It was Mike.

"One tomato and tuna," said the waitress, setting down Francesca's plate.

Two women were talking, to the right of Francesca. They sat at the curve of the counter and she could hear their voices quite plainly.

". . . then he went on drugs and hid himself behind draperies on a platform in the living room and wouldn't talk to me except by tape recorder. He would record hateful messages while I was out working to support him and then when I came home I'd open the front door and I'd hear this click and the voice would start in on me. I dreaded opening that door, but in a way, you know, I was curious to hear what the voice had to say each evening. It was a little like being hypnotized. Then, one day, went in and ordered a tuna fish sandwich and a glass of tea. Someone had left a paper on the table, it was called *The Village Voice*. She leafed through it. There was a want ad section. She scanned the employment notices. Most of them called for some skill.

Cartoonist. Must have portfolio . . .

Wanted Polynesian girl to dance at private party . . .

Typist half time on weekends and holidays, some knowledge of Mandarin . . .

Amanuensis needed. Personable, energetic.

BATHER & FLUFFER WANTED

What exactly was an amanuensis? Perhaps the skill was hidden in the meaning of that word. Francesca noted down the telephone number anyway. Perhaps she would try it later.

She realized she would have to return sooner or later to her dreary little room. She began walking slowly down the avenue, ticking off the blocks, feeling worse and worse. The tempo of the city was speeding up. There were more people hurrying up and down the sidewalks, stepping off the curbs to flag taxis. Everyone seemed sealed firmly into his life, urgently en route to some destination, rushing toward someone waiting somewhere.

Why was she here, subjecting herself to these terrors?

Ah. She was leaving Cameron, whom she did not love, to start a new life, to open herself to possibilities.

I said, 'Fuck this, I can call myself names as well as any tape recorder,' and that was the end of that."

"What kind of names did he call you?"

"Oh the usual. Fat cow. Lying cunt. Nothing very imaginative."

Francesca began to feel better. The tuna salad was good, though not as tasty as the one Cameron made, and things looked more hopeful. She finally felt well enough to look across the counter at her reflection in the mirror. She stood out, a definitely beautiful woman in this lunchtime mob of women. She decided to find a hairdresser immediately after lunch, to rectify the big difference between herself and Nina Brett, and perhaps after that she would try one more employment agency. What was the hurry? She still had plenty of traveler's checks, and if worse came to worse there was Cameron's fat bank draft at First National, waiting for her. But she mustn't touch that, she had promised Mike. Suddenly she saw Mike as someone not to be trusted. Why? It was as though he really had betrayed her for smooth Nina Brett.

"I just hate my hair lately," she was telling Jacques, some fifteen or twenty minutes later. He was the manager of a very attractive salon with black dryers and a crimson carpet and a huge fish tank with exotic, tropical fish. When Francesca had wandered in, the girl at the desk said nobody could possibly take her till three. Francesca had noticed the small, dapper man with the Van Dyke, slouching beside his fish tank, watching her out of the corner of his eye. Then suddenly there he was beside her. "I will take Madam," he said. The girl at the desk was surprised, especially when Jacques himself led Francesca to the row of basins where mere apprentices shampooed other ladies and washed her hair with his own hands.

"You have excellent hair. A pleasure to work with. All this thin, damaged stuff one sees . . . I am disgusted sometimes. So why do you hate your hair?" Slouched forward behind her chair, he sucked in his cheeks and experimented with his comb.

"Yes, I like it close to my head, like that. Oh, I don't know. It's been so frazzly and overblown. I want it tight and proper and . . . disciplined."

"You want to look like a nun," Jacques said.

They both laughed. Francesca wondered if he was queer.

"Yes. Maybe you could make it into a sort of knot . . . after it's dry . . . here on the back of my neck."

"And your husband, how will he like this nun?"

"Oh he—lets me do what I want." Jacques must have noticed her rings. Perhaps she should take them off for the next employment agency. And call herself Miss.

"He is a clever man."

Jacques handblew her hair dry himself, sensuously drawing his fingers through the strands. "Now we will let it cool a little. I don't want to damage it with the brush." While her masses of clean hair cooled, Jacques took a small green bottle and shook a couple of drops in his palms which he then rubbed energetically together. Francesca watched him anoint her head, this precise little man who was sometimes disgusted by other women's

hair. She felt oddly treasured by him and was happy th[at] her hair pleased him.

"Are you and your husband visiting, or do you li[ve] here?"

"We are visiting." She thought Jacques would pre[fer] her to have this clever husband beside her in the ci[ty.]

"That means you will dine out tonight, yes?"

"Yes. I guess we will."

"Good. I know just what I am going to do with yo[ur] hair. It will be a compromise between the nun and . . . *haute coiffure*. It will be a chaste elegance. Your husba[nd] will die of admiration."

Shortly after three, Francesca reappeared on the sid[e]walk of the city. Her appearance no longer displeased he[r.] Jacques had made the top and sides of her head a slee[k] coppery-black skull cap. From the front, she was as tidy [as] any Nina Brett. In the back coiled two thick, sinuous plait[s] into which Jacques had woven a thin black velvet ribbo[n.] "I wish I could be there when you walk in," Jacques ha[d] said. He had offered to do the braids for her agai[n] tomorrow or the next day, for as long as she would be i[n] the city. Such a proud, touching man. Perhaps she woul[d] come back.

It came as a shock when she remembered her rea[l] predicament. There was no one waiting for her in thi[s] city, no one to die of admiration when she walked int[o] a room with her new look. She was so disappointed tha[t] she could not make up her mind to try another agenc[y] just yet. Besides, all the good jobs would probably b[e] filled by afternoon. She found another restaurant an[d]

Did Mike love her? Would she ever see him again? Would he come back next weekend? Would she have a job? Mrs. Michael Reusing . . . Rushing . . .

What would Cameron do, when he realized she was leaving him? Come after her, try to drag her back? Would he plead? Would he weep?

She could not imagine Cameron weeping.

How was she going to get through the next seventeen hours, until it was time to call Nina Brett back and ask were there any jobs yet?

What was an amanuensis? If only Cameron were here. He knew all sorts of tricky words. The job would probably be filled by now anyway.

Are you and your husband visiting? That means you will dine out tonight, yes?

Francesca stopped for a WAIT light. Suddenly her heart leapt. Who was facing her, an impatient frown on her chalk-pale face, just across this street, but Nina Brett! Her slim body in prison-matron gray pressed forward with the crowd which would, any minute now, be surging toward Francesca. She was wearing large sunglasses, but Francesca was almost positive Nina was looking directly at her. She smiled tentatively, a little embarrassed at her pleasure. How glad she was she had found Jacques.

The WAIT changed to WALK. Shyly, Francesca lowered her eyes and moved toward the other girl. Nina Brett, the only other person, besides Jacques, she knew in this city. Perhaps Nina would ask her to supper. She must remember to ask about Nina's cat.

When they were almost touching, in the middle of the street, Francesca cried, "Hello, again!" Nina looked startled, pressed her red lips tighter together, and moved quickly past. Francesca saw the girl's eyes briefly flick over her, then away. Stunned by this obvious cut, she did not repeat her greeting and Nina soon disappeared.

"How stupid of me. Of course she didn't see me. The sun was in her eyes."

Francesca turned the corner and saw her hotel. It looked so shabby, so impoverished. She would go inside and take the elevator to the third floor and unlock that dark-brown potbellied door. When she closed it behind her, it would be as though she ceased to be. Nobody in this city, nobody in the entire universe—not even Mike, who had never seen her in this room—could imagine her inside it.

"Also, she probably didn't recognize me with this new hair style."

12 ANOTHER INTERVIEW

Nine fourteen a.m. Monday, Pacific time. Jerry Freeman, breathing hard from his run upstairs (he was late and couldn't wait for the elevator) found a note from the Managing Editor stuck under the bar of his typewriter.

Jerry: Pls see me
Eric N.

Did that mean now? Jerry looked across the city room, cluttered with desks, people, and typewriters, to the cool glassed-in office where the Managing Editor sat alone in his immaculate shirtsleeves. The Managing Editor waved at Jerry. He'd been watching the whole time, waiting. And Jerry had come in almost fifteen minutes late, a rare transgression. *Do you mean see you now?* Jerry mimed. The Managing Editor gave a cordial nod. Jerry started to shrug off his jacket and hang it on the back of his chair. Then he thought better of this and started across the room, working his way through the desks, toward the glass office. Jerry had so far entered this office twice. The first time was June of fourteen months ago, when he'd been taken on as a summer intern, after his graduation from journalism school. The second time was in September, when he had been informed by the Managing Editor that he had made the team. "You have a way with language," the Managing Editor had said, "and a nice straightforward way of looking at things. We like that."

Jerry had carefully deposited these two compliments in the upper reaches of his memory. In the months to follow, he drew on them again and again to restore his flagging energies and enthusiasm for unspectacular assignments, to remind himself exactly why he was valuable. He wrote and re-wrote his reports of tedious port authority meetings, dehydrating them of superfluities till they, unlike the real meetings, crackled with crispness. He worked overtime to find in the most depressing assignments (the opening of a new home for paraplegics; a blind octogenarian ex-cop who had won a baking contest) something true, even visionary. He kept a thesaurus in his desk and went about training himself to look upon everything with clarity. Language and vision. He so wanted to be excellent.

Why did the Managing Editor want to see him? Had he done anything wrong? At this point in his career, Jerry threaded his way between peaks of hubris and pits of inferiority.

"Mr. Neuhoffer?"

"Hi, Jerry. Have a seat. How have things been going?"

"Fine. I've been working hard."

"I'm happy to hear you find the two things synonymous."

"How are *you*?" said Jerry, then wished he hadn't, because the Managing Editor was opening his mouth to say something else.

"I'm fine, too. Jerry, what do you know about District Attorney Bolt?"

"I've seen him a couple of times on TV. That's about all. I know he's got a reputation for being rigidly conservative. I don't know much more."

"That's fine, Jerry."

"I beg your pardon."

"That's all you need to know. Let me explain what we have in mind. Bolt's expected to announce his candidacy for Attorney General at a dinner next week, when his wife returns. She's off in the east on a shopping trip. What we need now, for Sunday's Feature section, is a personality profile of the man. Something like you did on that blind cop. Talk to him, listen to him, see what there is to see. Then come back and write down your impressions."

"I'll have to do some research . . ."

"I'd set up the interview as soon as possible. Deadline

for Sunday features is Thursday. You might glance over what we've got on him in the morgue. But what I'm primarily after are your impressions." He stood up, sucked in his stomach, and centered his belt buckle. He was a medium-sized, hard-fleshed, stocky man with very bright eyes behind those silver-rimmed glasses. His hair was thick, a mixture of black and silver. What does he think of me, Jerry wondered, both afraid and envious of this man whose meteoric career was discussed reverently by other staff members. But Neuhoffer was a man with the reputation of wasting neither time nor words. Jerry understood this interview was over.

He went back to his own desk, feeling a bit light-headed. Conversations with Neuhoffer always affected him like this, even if it was only a two-minute conversation about the weather on the elevator. He took off his jacket and sat down at his desk, aware that the Managing Editor might be watching him through the glass. He took out a clean steno pad and jotted down some words he had no need of jotting down. While he did this, he re-ran the conversation in his mind to see if he had said anything stupid. No. Not really. Then he picked up the phone and asked the operator to get the District Attorney's office for him. He sensed her annoyance. Why couldn't he look it up himself and dial? He didn't want to be seen by Neuhoffer flipping uncertainly through the pages. He set up a one fifteen appointment with Bolt's secretary, then snatched up his steno pad and hurried to the morgue, where he sat, ignoring coffee breaks, ignoring lunch, poring over the District Attorney's thick envelope of clippings. Bolt didn't give away much about his personal life.

The most personal thing about him, as far as Jerry could glean from this packet of newsprint, was that he was married to a beautiful woman. Jerry spent some time looking at a photograph of this wife, taken a year ago for a Women's feature.

What was he going to say about Cameron Bolt? What would his impressions of the man be? But he mustn't try to predict them. He must go to this interview without preconceptions. Still, he wanted to go to it without handicaps, to do a stunning piece of work.

He went through the clippings again, jotting down words and phrases of Bolt's.

"I confess to being a patriot and a perfectionist, yes."

"And so, in the name of freedom, they are permitted to kill one another on the streets. *Cui bono?*"

"Do I cavil, gentlemen? If so, it is not to waste your valuable time, I assure you, but to give Justice time to pick up her skirts and run like the wind to join us here in this courtroom."

There were several editorials concerning Bolt. One was on the subject of Crystal Gardens, the much-discussed hangout for the misguided young. The writer felt that the District Attorney had deliberately put this place on show in order to hasten public disgust with the prevailing climate of permissiveness.

"We are not saying that the District Attorney has not come to terms with the present age because he lacks the capacity to recognize its seriousness. We are saying he refuses to recognize its existence because he disdains its style."

Who wrote that editorial? Could Neuhoffer have written it?

There were some cartoons depicting the political career of Cameron Bolt. In one, the artist had drawn an apocalyptic figure on horseback, riding across a tumultuous sky, brandishing a broom. In another, he stood in an art gallery, slouched in front of a huge canvas filled with war, race riots, starving figures, flames, and great smoky clouds of smog. Arms folded, eyes narrowed in a connoisseur's squint, Bolt was saying, "That picture, gentlemen, has become the great national bore."

What kind of story did Neuhoffer expect from him? What did he want to see?

If Neuhoffer himself were interviewing Cameron Bolt, what kind of story would he write?

Jerry went to the N's and slipped out Neuhoffer's bulging envelopes. He had two. It was the policy of the paper to keep everything written by any staff member. Jerry himself had a slim envelope, which he checked frequently, comparing his progress to the young Neuhoffer's, who had joined this paper as an intern also, become City Editor within four years and Managing Editor in six more.

Jerry arranged the envelopes so they could be instantly covered by the steno pad if someone (if Neuhoffer himself!) happened to stroll through the morgue and peek over Jerry's shoulder. He did not want to be caught in the act of studying another man's success.

He reviewed Neuhoffer's famous "series" which had put him, as a young reporter of twenty-four, in the limelight: eight articles which methodically stripped the masks from a network of swindlers who made their living off people's religious beliefs. Jerry went over each article, noting the staccato syntax, rich in verbs, sparing of modifiers, which rapped on, sharp and inexorable as the teletype machine, piling fact on fact till the point was made as clearly as that little bell that went *bing-bing-bing*, signaling the end of a story.

Perhaps his own story, this interview with Cameron Bolt, would, in years to come, be studied minutely, in secret, by some future young hopeful who had heard the tale of how Jerry Freeman first came to prominence with his revealing profile of a District Attorney aspiring to be Attorney General, a piece of journalism remarkable for its insight into an age-old type of suppressive personality.

Jerry bowed his head over the desk covered with these fragments of two men's lives and pressed his fists hard against his eyelids. He was feeling a little dizzy. Skipping lunch, probably. He'd only had a cup of coffee for breakfast. The morgue was hot. What time was it?

Jerry shot up, dismayed. This mess of newspaper clippings! Which belonged to Neuhoffer, which to Bolt? Mumbling "Neuhoffer . . . Neuhoffer . . . Bolt, Bolt . . . no, Neuhoffer" he frantically stuffed the envelopes. His interview with Bolt was in ten minutes! How had this possibly happened? He felt as if, somewhere during the course of his reading, he had slipped into some sinister time zone with laws all its own.

"Mr. Freeman? How do you do? I'm Cameron Bolt." The two men shook hands in the anteroom of Bolt's cool, spacious offices in front of a watchful secretary. Jerry hoped his hand was not sticky. He had run most of the way to this interview, there had not been a taxi in sight. He was shocked to see Bolt had colors, after studying so many black and white images of the man. His hair, which he wore very short except for a boyish slab that fringed forward across one temple, was a mixture of reddish and silver; his eyes a green-gray. His rough-textured skin was tanned a yellowish-brown. Jerry recalled a small clipping about Bolt's golf game. He wore a well-fitting suit of soft blue-gray against a shirt of exactly the same color. A deep blue tie with a thin slanting red stripe completed this ensemble.

"I'm glad to see you are young and energetic," said Cameron Bolt, "because I'd like to take a walk. I've been in meetings since eight this morning. We can talk as we walk. Would you mind?"

"A walk would be great," said Jerry, still breathing fast from his run. He reasoned that Bolt walking might show him more sides than Bolt sitting down in his office.

They went down together in the elevator. Bolt looked directly at Jerry, as though he were conducting a private interview of the younger man. His mouth was fixed in a bland, meditative smile. Jerry returned the smile, then looked away, pretending to watch the descending numbers above the door. Out of the corner of his eye, he saw Bolt clasp his yellow-brown hands around a phantom golf club and swing lightly from the wrist.

They reached the ground floor. "You play golf a lot, don't you?" said Jerry for openers.

"Alas, not as much as I'd like. Not these days."

"Do you play any other sports? Tennis? Squash?"

"No," said the other dreamily, turning left on the side-walk. "Golf is my game."

"Why is that? Is it the setting you like, or the people you play with, or what?"

The District Attorney, setting a quick, skimming stride that made Jerry step up his own, appeared to be thinking this over.

"I find it satisfying. It is a game in which I compete with myself and judge myself. On the golf course, I am my own constituency of one."

Jerry made a mental note of the sentence.

"But you play against other people, don't you?"

"Sometimes yes. Sometimes no. But it is always my own score I am striving to beat."

Jerry saw a possible analogy which might propel them out of this *Sports Illustrated* chit-chat. "Would you say that you felt similarly about the forthcoming competition for which you are expected to declare next week?

The District Attorney slowed down. "Yes," he said, look-ing at Jerry with interest. "That's right. I'm interested in finding the most challenging and most complete use for my capacities. The notion of competition doesn't interest me. Measuring myself against other players is not my game at all. I like that. I must remember it."

Jerry felt gratified as the man neatly pocketed his own ideas. He wished he had eaten lunch. His face was damp and his heart pounding crazily.

"Does the label 'extremist-conservative' bother you, Mr. Bolt?"

"Only because it hasn't been carried to its last extreme.

I would like to be identified with the final form of that quality, like one of Plato's eternal *eidos*. I would like to be The Conservator personified. You know of course what a conservator is?"

"One who conserves . . .?"

Bolt smiled. "Go on."

"I guess I can't. Not on the spur of the moment, anyway," admitted Jerry.

"Very few can. The poor word and its derivatives have become so muddied over with contemporary cant. What a shame our young people are no longer required to learn Latin in high school. No wonder they are ignorant of their *own* roots. 'He's conservative,' they say, when they mean he's stuffy, out-of-date, 'up-tight.' There is not the remotest connection between the meanings! Even my wife, Francesca, who knows better, sometimes asks me, 'You don't think this dress is too conservative, do you?' She means all buttoned up, something thick and clumsy which would obscure her natural loveliness. I don't consider myself stuffy or all buttoned up at all." He gave a modest laugh. "At least I hope I don't seem so. I do hope I seem what I am. A conservator. A guardian, a protector of living forms. And, as you said, one who conserves or preserves, keeps things from being damaged, wasted, lost."

"Like energy," Jerry heard himself say. The words had simply popped out, pushed from beneath by the pressure of his concerns.

"You're inspiring, Mr. Freeman." Once again, Jerry had the sense that his own words were being stored away in Bolt's orderly memory for later use. "Certainly like energy. As long as we have energy, we can see things clearly. We aren't caught off-balance by our own fears or needs. Decrease it, you have muddleheaded men who don't know what they want, what they mean. Take it away altogether and you have slaves. Energy is crucial to any accomplishment. I have been blessed with so much myself. At the end of the day I have so much left over that I do the housework when I get home."

"You do—"

Cameron Bolt laughed. He walked faster, he almost floated down the sidewalk. Jerry hurried along beside him, feeling damp all over now.

"Few men would admit to such a thing, much less do it. But I like it. I enjoy it. I find it an accompaniment to meditation. Waxing a floor is no different from turning a prayer wheel. And it saves my wife's beauty and energy."

"You'll certainly get the women's vote, if that gets out," said Jerry.

"I suppose it will get out," mused Bolt, turning abruptly into the gates of the notorious Crystal Gardens. "Let's find a quiet place, sit down for a bit."

"A quiet place? *Here*?"

"Sure," said Cameron. "The only noise is inside their heads."

Jerry tried not to stare as Bolt led them through clusters of half-clothed bodies lying about on the grass. Several of them raised a dreamy peace sign at Bolt, who acknowledged them with a crisp smile and the upturned flat of his hand. "I wish they would stop building fires in the grass," he said. "See those black ruined places? I had a number of outdoor fireplaces put in, just like the state parks, but I suppose they feel that would compromise them." Bolt

sat down on the shady part of a bench, beneath a eucalyptus tree, leaving Jerry the sunny side. Jerry's stomach
rumbled and concluded with a loud squeal. He leaned
forward against his folded arms, embarrassed.

"How do you feel about . . . what a lot of people are
saying about this park? That it is your showpiece to
dampen liberal enthusiasms."

"Your paper's editorials haven't attributed me with the
greatest humanitarianism. Of course the existence of Crystal Gardens is bound to alienate many people. I'm aware
of that. Just as these people," he swept a yellow-brown
hand across the park, "are aware that it is much easier for
our State Bureau of Narcotics to find them gathered here
in broad daylight, or under bright stars, rather than
scattered in dark little cubbyholes all over the city. But
here they are, all the same. Why do you think that is, Mr.
Freeman? I think it may have something to do with our
remarks a few minutes ago about energy. These people
don't have much of that commodity to spare. Also, I think
they have that sense peculiar to children of wanting to be
looked after. I think that when they have shot themselves
too full of nightmares they allow themselves to be caught.
Just as a child will cry out and wake his parents in the
night. So we come and comfort them. We remove them
from their nightmares."

"Put them in jail, you mean."

"When one is expelled, or expels himself from the
Garden, Mr. Freeman, the next step is not Heaven . . . it
is Purgatory. Some make it out of Purgatory eventually.
Not many, mind you, but some." Bolt sniffed. "I must say,
Paradise is not all that fresh today."

Now Jerry smelled it. The odor of too many unwashed bodies, dogs, other things. So many of them out there, lying and dreaming in the sun, like soiled lilies of the field. Jerry watched a girl, who looked scarcely more than a child, lift her loose smock and drag out a breast with a dark, discolored nipple and fasten an infant to it.

"Soiled lilies of the field," he said aloud, then realized he was angling for another compliment from the District Attorney.

"What a wordsmith you are, Mr. Freeman. Your paper must feel lucky to have you. Like the rest of the culture, journalism has degenerated to the expressing of itself in a handful of slogans. The vocabulary of everyone is dwindling, don't you find that?"

"Yes," said Jerry, who was not feeling very well at all. Several yards away, the baby sucked and the noises were making Jerry's empty stomach queasy. What if he should vomit in front of Bolt? He wondered if his paper did feel "lucky to have him." Sweat trickled down the sides of his body. Could he move over into Bolt's shade?

"However, they are not exactly arrayed to outdo Solomon in all his glory," said Bolt.

Jerry's nausea was now replaced by a light, effervescent sensation in his neck and face. It was a moist bubble which might detach itself and float away at any moment, simply dance away on the current of the District Attorney's musing, precise little speeches. The clusters of bodies did seem to waver and sway like lilies on stalks. Over on the grass, the baby made certain noises. The girl plucked him from her breast, laid him down on the grass, and unfastened his diaper.

"I won't deny its legal convenience," Bolt continued. "Many in this crowd are due to show up in court sometime soon. If any of them forget—and memory cells don't function too well in crystal gardens—we can simply drop by and remind them. No reason why these conveniences shouldn't work both ways."

Jerry closed his eyes to keep from watching the girl swab the baby's bottom. At that moment, humanity seemed sickening, awful. He saw a ghastly vision of himself, striving for a place above all this mess, crawling along through miles and miles of exactly what was coming out of that baby's bottom, trying to keep from choking as he enunciated *bon mot* after *bon mot,* trying to keep his vision clean, in order that he might arrive at that exalted day when he, too, would sit on the shady side of a bench and have his every word attended to, or inside a glass cubicle, controlling by a mere bright-eyed glance, a few words on a piece of scrap paper ("Pls see me—the ME"), the days of other people. He bowed his head in his hands, feeling faint.

"Mr. Freeman, is anything wrong?"

"I'm not sure," muttered Jerry, bowing his head as low as he could, without appearing ridiculous. He had read somewhere that this position sent the blood back to your head. "The heat is a little . . . I skipped lunch. Also that . . . disgusting smell."

"Can you walk? We'll get a cab just outside the gate."

"I don't know if I can or not," Jerry almost sobbed.

"Yes you can. Look at me, Freeman."

Jerry, with some effort, lifted his head and looked at

Bolt. His eyes were a cool gray-green. There was something fanatic about his face.

"Let's try an experiment. Let me transfer some of my
energy to you. I have a surplus at the moment. Here. Take
what you need."

He is mad, thought Jerry. He has delusions of super-
natural powers. He really believes he is more than other
men. And as Jerry looked closely at the face of this man,
he had a moment of utter clarity, the kind which confirms
a correct intuition. *This is the real challenge of this assign-
ment*, he realized, *to be able to render this man so that
people will feel what I am experiencing now, right now.
Both the attraction and the danger.* He saw Neuhoffer
sitting in that cool glass office and turning the pages of his
own story slowly, in wonderment, amazement.

Yet he was walking calmly beside Bolt toward the exit
of the Gardens. "You look much better," said Bolt. "I'll
find a cab."

"No, please. I can walk. I feel fine. It seems to have
passed." He did feel remarkably fine. *Could* this man have
effected some sort of energy transfer? Perhaps he was a
hypnotist.

Back in the District Attorney's office, Bolt said, "You
don't value your own energies highly enough, Mr. Freeman. You shouldn't have skipped lunch. I'm not saying
that we should all sit down and stuff ourselves every noon
hour. But there are times to fast and times to eat. A man
with an empty stomach has very little resistance to the
unexpected. I happened to skip lunch today myself, and
that was foolish of me. Why don't I have some sand-

wiches sent up now? We both need to eat and then we can wind up the interview."

"That would be . . . very nice," said Jerry, sinking at the District Attorney's gesture into a comfortable black leather chair. This office was bereft of personal touches.

Bolt perched on the edge of his immaculate desk and spoke into the intercom to his secretary. He swung his legs slightly. The thin ankles in their black socks looked incongruous performing this casual motion. "I'll have a hot pastrami on pumpernickel with Dutch mustard, not too much, a side order of sauerkraut, a side order of potato salad, a linzer torte, and black coffee," he said. He knew exactly what he wanted, this man. "And Mr. Freeman will have . . ." He looked up at Jerry. "What will you have?"

"That sounds fine," said Jerry, who did not feel up to making a decision at the moment.

"Mr. Freeman and I will have the same," Bolt said into the intercom.

13 ROOM 311

Monday evening, 8 p.m.

Dear Cameron,

I am in room 311 of this hotel. Don't be fooled by the picture on the stationery. It could never have looked this good, even thirty years ago. 311 is exactly ten by eighteen paces, counting detours around the furniture:

1. *A single bed that slopes to the right, as you lie in it. Cheap green spread.*
2. *An ugly dresser with a mirror which makes me look wobbly.*

3. *An ugly chair. Wooden arms. Faded mustard cushions.*
4. *An old TV, black and white. I watched part of a documentary on Senior Citizens in America, then got depressed and turned it off.*

311 is next to 313. The two rooms share a bath. There is something wrong with the girl in 313. The walls are thin and I can hear her talking wildly on the telephone, calling one number after another, and crying and shouting into the phone. They aren't thin enough for me to hear what she's saying. Then she runs into our bathroom and cries softly and has diarrhea. Now she's back on the phone. I wonder what her problem is?

You would hate this room, you would not stay in it a minute. It is a room for failures and lonely people. I am looking around it and seeing it through your eyes. Dull, unaesthetic colors. Cheap textures. Burned and scratched surfaces. Smell of dust, radiator pipes, old, worn out things. You would not even sit down. You would look around, sniff, and say . . . what would you say? I can see you standing in the middle of this little room, slouching back and folding your arms, and I can see your eyes narrow and your lips purse, the way they do before you say exactly what you mean.

The window is dirty and there is no screen. That surprises me. It worries me. I wonder if the girl in 313 has a screen. What if her problem gets worse and there is that window which can be opened quite easily by a woman, and no screen. Could a person kill herself from just the third floor? That is my question. What would yours be? Could the hotel be sued for not protecting its guests with screens?

I met a very chic and interesting person today. Nina Brett. She has a cat named Alexander. I would love to see the two of you together.

> *Goodnight for now,*
> *Francesca*

Francesca read this letter over Tuesday morning. She was killing time till it became 9:30 and she could telephone Nina Brett. Writing the letter had served its purpose, it had got her through last night. By imagining an audience, even if it was only Cameron, she was able to document herself. There was certainly no need to mail it. Yet the thought of those four carefully penned pages (there were several good observations, she thought) going in the wastebasket bothered her. Well, she would not decide now. Call Nina Brett first. If Nina had a job for her, she would tear up this letter.

She had wakened with the garbage trucks and been unable to go back to sleep. The uncertainties of the day ahead hulked like physical presences in this shabby room filling with summer daylight and she felt as though she were waking *into* a nightmare rather than the other way around. It became necessary to create a little catechism to orient herself.

> Q. Why are you here?
> A. I am here to find a job.
> Q. What purpose will it serve?
> A. To free myself from a life with a man I
>   do not love, to achieve my independence
>   as a human being, and to open up possi-
>   bilities for a life with a man I do love.

9:30! But no, perhaps she should give Nina five more minutes, to powder her face a paler white in the LADIES, smooth back that knot, check her stockings. She didn't want to make Nina run down the hall and snatch up the phone angrily and already be hating the person at the other end.

9:35. Trembling, Francesca gave the number to the

switchboard operator. This was one of those hotels where you couldn't dial out yourself.

"Brett."

"Hello. This is Francesca Bolt."

"Who?"

"Francesca *Bolt*. You said to call you this morning. You know. I was in your office yesterday. Your cat got stuck and you had to go home."

"Oh. What can I do for you, Mrs. Bolt?"

"Well, you said to call you and there might be a job today."

"Look, Mrs. Bolt, I might as well level with you, there just aren't any jobs available for a person of your . . . specific needs at the time. This is a terrible time for jobs. People with training, with M.A.'s, with Ph.D.'s, can't get jobs. The other thing is, well, you aren't a very good risk. You aren't even legally separated from your husband. You even put down your California address on the application form . . ."

"That was a mistake. I meant to put this address. I have a room in a hotel. I rent a room by the week." Francesca's mouth had gone oddly dry and her lips kept getting stuck together.

"That's hardly better. What's to keep you from bolting —excuse the pun—the first moment things get bad? I'm sorry, Mrs. Bolt, but I've been in this business almost eight years now and I have an eye for certain things. I sympathize and I wish you luck. But there's nothing further I can do for you."

"Well, thank you."

"Not at all. Goodbye."

Francesca hung up. She went to the mirror and looked in. Her hair was still done up in Jacques' complicated plaits. They did not look so neat any more. Slowly she unplaited them. It took a long time. Then she brushed out her long hair, which now had little crimps in it and looked untidier than ever. She was already dressed. She took her room key and put it in her purse. Her fingers collided with a book of airmail stamps Cameron had given her, so that she would write to him regularly from Kate's. She tore out a stamp and put it on the envelope already addressed to him and sealed it. While waiting for the one elevator in service to creep down from the twenty-second floor, she paced back and forth, sniffing the damp, old smell of the hall, flapping the envelope in her hand as though weighing it. The elevator door opened sluggishly and a number of unfriendly faces glowered impatiently toward her. She popped the letter into the chute and hurried nervously into their ranks.

She had breakfast in the hotel coffee shop, going through the ads in the paper as she nibbled a pineapple Danish and sipped her coffee. There was the smart ad for Nina Brett's agency, secure within its double lines. Francesca was excluded from this box now.

A short, plump man of about forty, with baby pink skin and a receding chin which disappeared suddenly into his white turtleneck shirt, asked if he could share her booth. He was an ex-priest, just off the morning plane from Madison, Wisconsin. He was staying at this hotel. Was she? Which room? Francesca gave him the number of the room she and Michael had shared. The eager homeliness of the ex-priest made her value Mike all the more.

She told him her name was Kate Brett. "Any relation to the nurse?" he laughed. She didn't get it. "I noticed you were looking at the ads, are you looking for a job too?" he asked. She said no, she just found it interesting, reading the different qualifications. People were so different. "That's exactly why I left the priesthood. I wasn't getting to enough people. This collar," he hacked at the turtleneck, "Where this collar *was,* I should say, was like a wall between me and humanity. I'm here to look for a job in the media, starting this morning. Something in television, preferably. What I'd really like is to get a job as an on-the-road interviewer, like that guy on CBS." Francesca asked him if he had any experience. "Twenty-two years in the priesthood," he said, "and I really like people and that should count for something." Francesca excused herself. She left him her paper.

There was a Cosmetics shop off the lobby of the hotel. She went in and stood staring at a display of perfumes. The saleslady in her pink smock was busy rubbing something into a customer's wrist. "Now I don't want you to be alarmed, but what I'm giving you is a very light, light shade. Actually, when this is blended with your own skin tone, the resulting effect will be quite beautiful." The customer, a light-skinned Negro girl who towered over the saleslady, did not look convinced. She mumbled something and went out. The saleslady now accosted Francesca, who was testing a perfume on her wrist. "That's brand new, our new perfume. It's actually quite lovely. *Vogue* gave us a good writeup. It's a nice GREEN-y smell, like being out of doors."

"Yes," agreed Francesca, thinking it was a thin, synthetic smell. Suddenly she remembered herself and Kate, how long ago, was it *nine* years ago? trying on perfumes in a little shop in Paris. It had been autumn, a clear autumn day, and Francesca remembered the smells of that day: French cigarettes and strong-roasted coffee, and all of those perfumes, being unstoppered one after another by the laughing, elegant Kate, who knew everything about perfumes, how the best ones were made from the gray, waxish secretion of sperm whales, how a perfume would smell differently on different people, how it was better always to buy a number of small bottles, the fragrance kept its integrity longer. There was a new perfume that day, too, one of the big couture houses had just come out with it. Kate had allowed the proprietor to scratch the glass applicator on the back of her little finger (the only place left, they had tried so many) and then, holding her hand very carefully, she walked to the front of the shop and stood outside in the sun, until the scent was thoroughly dry. She had lifted her hand to her nostrils, inhaled deeply, thoughtfully. "Oui," she said to the proprietor, "C'est moi." She wore that perfume for years after, during the whole Jonathan era. It was a dry, crisp scent, a little like hay, but also heady and mysterious.

Francesca asked the saleslady in the pink smock for Kate's old perfume.

"Oh no, dear. We only carry our own."

Francesca thanked her and went across the lobby to the elevator. After the usual wait, she ascended to her own room. The door was open. Was someone waiting for her, sitting in the ugly mustard chair, having left the door open so as not to alarm her? Mike?

It was the maid, a thin, light brown woman with stiff black hair. "I'm sorry, honey, I thought you'd gone for the day," she said cheerfully, moving aside to make space for Francesca as she passed through the narrow corridor between dresser and bed. She was making Francesca's bed. "I'll be through in a minute. Rose Ann, the girl who does this floor, has got some kind of virus, and I've come down from twenty-five to help out."

Francesca sat down in the mustard chair and folded her hands in her lap. She wished the woman would finish and go. She was afraid she was going to cry.

"You staying here long?" the maid asked Francesca.

"Not long," Francesca said. She didn't want to open up any possibilities for a longer conversation than necessary. "Have you . . . worked here long?" she added, for politeness's sake.

"Sixteen years, honey. But that's nothing. Some of the people who live here have been here for thirty."

"You mean in this hotel?"

"Sure. Twenty-four and twenty-five are little apartments, you see. A room about as big as this, no, a little bigger, then an alcove and a little kitchenette, and a bath. One lady has lived on twenty-five for thirty years now. She and me are friends. I come back on Sundays, my day off, and eat with her. She can't stand to eat alone. We go to these fancy restaurants where they have two or three courses before the meat. She and her husband lived on twenty-five for all these years, till just last spring. Then he died. He was ninety. He willed his body to medical science. I sat with her the night all the calls were coming in. The phone would ring and it would be one doctor, telling her how good her husband's brain was. It was the brain of a fifty-year-old, he said. Then another doctor would call and say how good his kidneys were . . ."

"God," said Francesca.

"No, Mrs. King was pleased. As each call came in, she'd say to me, 'See, Bessie, what a good man he was.' He was awfully good to her. He did everything for her. You see, she came from a very rich family, even a Duke from England wanted to marry her, but she loved Mr. King. He was in the glove business, and did all right for years, then the glove business went bad. Nobody buys gloves any more. So they moved in here, which isn't cheap. But it's the service they like, the convenience to the shops. He would fix her breakfast in that little kitchenette and even wash out her panties at night. Once he said to me, 'Bessie, if anything happens to me, you must take care of Sheila. She is helpless, she can't do anything for herself.' The day after he died, the housekeeper and I had to go around sticking signs on the wall, telling her what to do. We made a sign for the stove, it's just two electric burners, saying TO TURN ON REAR BURNER, TURN RIGHT HAND KNOB TO RIGHT . . . TO TURN ON FRONT BURNER, TURN LEFT HAND KNOB TO RIGHT . . . She couldn't even open a 7-Up for herself, he always opened them for her and then mixed it with a little water, so it wouldn't be too strong. The first time she tried to heat a can of soup for herself on the stove, she put the can down on the burner and when it didn't get hot immediately put her hand down to see why. The doctor had to come. Do you want me to run the carpet sweeper, or had you rather be alone?"

"Don't bother about the carpet."

"Okay. How many towels you need? Two be enough?"

"Yes, thank you."

"Here you go, then. Rose ought to be back tomorrow. This virus is going around, but it doesn't last long. I didn't mean to talk your ear off."

"No, it was interesting. I certainly hope Mrs. King will be all right."

The maid laughed. "Oh, she'll be all right. She's got me to take care of her, she's got the whole staff to take care of her. When we die off, somebody else will take care of her. That kind always manages to get taken care of." She winked at Francesca and closed the door behind her.

Francesca lay down on the bed. She drew her legs up and closed her eyes. She did not move for a long time.

Eventually she got up, rummaged through her purse, and called the number on the slip of paper. A voice answered.

"I'm calling about your ad I saw in the paper yesterday."

"Oh. Are you interested?"

"I think I am. What exactly is an amanuensis? What skills do you have to have?" Francesca couldn't tell if she was speaking to a man or a woman.

"An amanuensis is someone who guards the privacy and serenity of a person who wants to get important work done. An amanuensis is quiet and even-tempered, writes letters, answers mail, pays bills, and does not object to a bit of light housecleaning."

"I could do all but the typing. I can't type."

"Who said anything about typing. There's only one typewriter here and I'm using that."

"Oh."

"Would you like to come over? We could discuss it better face to face."

"What is your address?"

The voice gave her the address. "Top floor."

"Will a taxi take me there?"

"Not to the top floor. Where are you now?"

"In the west fifties."

"Well, if you leave now, you should be here in about fifteen minutes. My name is Evans. What is yours?"

"Francesca Bolt."

"Well, Francesca Bolt, see you shortly."

"Yes. Well, goodbye . . ."

"Goodbye."

Francesca sat on the edge of the bed and nibbled a cuticle. Evans what? Or was it Something Evans? Well, at least she had a reason to leave this room. She counted her cash and traveler's checks. Fourteen dollars in cash and some change. A hundred and sixty left in traveler's checks. Where had she spent so much money? It seemed impossible. At the end of the week, the first fifty-two dollars on this room would be due. She might make it on what she had for two weeks. But not if the dollars kept slipping away, unaccounted for.

14   M EVANS

The two women stared at each other. Francesca, panting
from the nine flights of stairs in this stifling building, tried
not to appear shocked by her prospective employer.

"Miss Evans?"

"*M* Evans. Come in."

M or Em Evans had a large, plain face of uncertain age.
Her wide, pale-blue eyes focused avidly on Francesca,
taking in her face, her hair, her body, with shameless
thoroughness. She wore a black muu-muu, beneath which

breasts were faintly discernible. These were Francesca's only evidence of gender, for M or Em had shaved her head.

"Well, come in."

There were several rooms opening into one another, railroad style. All were in a mess, strewn with papers, books, clothes, and . . . a variety of broken china which had been kicked or brushed to the corners of the rooms. Francesca's nostrils quivered. Something smelled rotten.

"I'll just clear out this chair," said the other, gathering up a handful of books and papers.

"Is the . . . uh . . . Em short for Emily? Emma?" asked Francesca, wondering how quickly she could sit down and get up and get out again. The smell . . .

"No. It's my posthumous name. It stands for me, the pure, uncluttered, anonymous me. I have died to the world for all practical purposes and now I am trying to become anonymous, transparent. Sit down."

"Is it some sort of religion, then?" Francesca sat down.

"You could call it that." M went behind a table piled high with books and papers and covered with a floor-length cloth. She sat down so suddenly that it appeared as though her head had been cut off and placed on the table with the books and papers. Francesca could see past the head to the kitchen sink at the end of the third room. It was filled with pots and dishes. She began thinking up excuses to go. She looked back at M, who smiled, showing a strong set of gap-teeth.

"Let me try and read the thoughts of Francesca Bolt," said M. "Recently, she arrived in this city, full of hope and vitality. But the hope and vitality are dwindling. Things are not as she expected. She sees her reflection in windows, but not in the loving eyes of friends. She has begun to have moments in which she doubts reality. She stumbles into places where the rules have changed, or else where things seem mad. Now she is trapped in one of these places and wonders how soon she can get out without being rude. This person who answered the door is the strangest person she has ever seen. Might be a religious freak, a sexual pervert, perhaps a murderer even. Also, the surroundings are not very clean. Francesca is used to better. She feels she has wasted an hour of her life, and taxi fare, and nine flights of stairs' worth of oxygen. Am I close?"

"How do you . . . know all that?"

"I'm getting so much better," remarked M, obviously pleased. "I think shaving my head helped some."

"Why did you do it?"

"So I would stop looking into the mirror. That surprises you. But I'll tell you something I'll bet you didn't know. Ugly women look in the mirror much more frequently than beautiful ones."

Francesca was dying to ask why, but thought it would be unpleasant for M to dwell on such a painful subject. So she asked, "If I took the job, what exactly would I have to do?"

"I won't beat around the bush. First: clean up this filthy apartment. Second: do something about my nutrition. Third: catch up with all my correspondence and last month's bills. Since my last . . . amanuensis left, I haven't gone out at all, and things have piled up. Now, how much do you think I should pay you? You can probably do everything in one or two days a week. Does thirty sound fair?"

"Thirty," repeated Francesca, stunned.

"Thirty a week, I mean. Not month," M explained generously.

"I'm afraid I would need more than that," Francesca said. "I mean, the weekly rent on my room alone is fifty-two. And I have to eat . . ."

"Oh, you're looking for a full-time job," said M. "I'm afraid this is only part-time. I usually get young people, students, you know, who want a little pocket money. I thought you were one of those. No, what you should do is go to a good employment agency."

Francesca burst into tears.

M said nothing. She watched with steady wide eyes until Francesca collected herself. Then she said, "You had better tell me all. Then we can think what to do."

An hour later, Francesca was wheeling a cart happily around a neighborhood supermarket, purchasing staples for M's kitchen with her own money. M did not have a cent in the house, she explained, having stayed inside ever since she shaved her head. This action had taken place three weeks ago. If Francesca could just do a bit of cleaning today and get some food in, then M said tomorrow they could see their way clear to financial contingencies. She promised to reimburse Francesca as soon as she found her checkbook. It had been agreed that Francesca could be temporary amanuensis to M while continuing to search for a full-time job. Or, M hoped, Francesca could find a second part-time job to supplement the weekly thirty dollars and continue on with M. M said in her opinion it was extremely important for Francesca to stay occupied. "You'll be less tempted to bolt back to Bolt, as that Brett creature predicted," said M. Francesca had confided about her plans to leave Cameron and her unsatisfying job-hunting up until now. She had given a pretty complete story, except for Mike. Somehow she did not feel it to her advantage to tell M there was a Mike.

Now she bought bread, cheese, instant coffee, apples, a ham salad spread, a pair of yellow rubber gloves exactly like the ones Cameron had, a large container of scouring powder, some dishwashing liquid, four rolls of toilet paper, two dishcloths, a spray can of lemon-scented furniture polish and a spray can of room freshener. She was enjoying herself! During those last apathetic months in California, she had given up shopping altogether. Cameron had taken over: he found no fault with his own selections, whereas she had occasionally irritated him by coming home with an inferior cut of meat, the wrong kind of marmalade, an unripe Camembert, a too-hard avocado. But she felt sure M would not notice such things and the freedom to choose carelessly gave her a pleasing sense of responsibility. Poor M! How had she survived for a month in that mess, with only stale fruitcake and frankfurters (everything else in the refrigerator was rotten), using old magazines as toilet paper? Already, Francesca was planning the ordering of M's contingent life, as M called it, so M could get on with her Project. This Project, which M had outlined for her briefly, fascinated Francesca. M was postulating a small cast of extraordinary personalities, drawing from biographies, novels, magazine and TV profiles, newspaper articles, collecting and combining "the most desirable traits" of persons in real life and fiction. The mere assembling of M's elite cast would take her months, perhaps years, of devoted, single-minded labor. That is why she could not be bothered with contingencies like buying food and paying bills and cleaning her apartment. When the cast was assembled, M would then build a world for them to live in. It would be in the form of a story, but the more perspicacious of readers would discern that this story was also a blueprint for the Desirable World, the way things should be. "Do you think people will want to follow the blueprint?" Francesca had asked. "It would be *nice* if they did," said M, "but if they don't, I will at least have kept myself busy."

Feeling expansive, Francesca added to her grocery cart a package of dried apricots (M could nibble on them while working and they were nutritious) and a five-dollar bottle of all-purpose vitamins. When she departed from the store, she had spent almost all of a twenty-dollar traveler's check. She walked back to M's, sweating in her good dress under the load of groceries. Such an interesting neighborhood. So many kinds of people. She smiled over her paper bags at a man in a lavender shirt and tight green pants, walking his dog. He did not smile back. Oh well! She had plenty to do. Her mind raced ahead. Put away the food, clean the kitchen, perhaps start on the bathroom ... Yesterday afternoon, when Nina Brett had snubbed her on that other street, seemed very far away. She turned into

M's building and climbed the nine flights of stairs carrying the two heavy bags. In California, going down in the elevator had become a chore.

M had dragged out her typewriter and was busily clattering away. "I feel so much better!" she cried to Francesca. "Already I feel less tyrannized by the contingent life!"

"Would you like some lunch?" asked Francesca.

M's bald head nodded yes. The hair was starting to come back, a very light fuzz forming like moss on a rock.

Francesca prepared ham salad sandwiches (she had forgotten to buy mayonnaise) and sliced apples. Where were the plates? Rather than disturb M's typing, she served lunch on a folded piece of typing paper.

"I can't seem to find the plates."

"I smashed them all," said M, not missing a beat in her typing.

Francesca went back to the kitchen. She had made a sandwich for herself, but was too excited to eat. There was so much to do. She started cleaning out the refrigerator, throwing away rotting carrots, old containers of mildewed cottage cheese, a carton of sour milk that made her retch. Soon the trash bin was almost full. She must remember to buy some of those plastic liners Cameron used. In the middle of one job, she would suddenly notice some other job that seemed more urgent. The kitchen window. The first time she saw it, she had assumed it looked out on a black wall, but now she saw, making a wet circle with her finger, that it looked down on a very charming street scene. Overjoyed, she set at once to washing it with dish washing liquid and one of the new cloths. It soon became black, so she used the other. She would buy more cloths tomorrow, and mayonnaise, paper plates, perhaps a little plant to hang in the clean window and brighten things up more. The effect of the clean window was to her the equivalent of a small miracle. Wait till M saw how bright everything was. Oh but how' awful the floor looked now. She must buy a can of floor wax tomorrow. What was the one Cameron used? He fussed if she got anything else. It came in a red and blue can, that's all she could remember. She wanted to get down on her knees now and start scrubbing this floor. But her skirt was too tight and there were no more cloths. Tomorrow she would wear pants.

On to the bathroom. M typed madly. Francesca felt the two of them were mutually engaged on a worthwhile afternoon. She put in the new roll of toilet paper. Tried and failed to clean the mirror. Someone had soaped it and the soap had dried hard. Buy sponges tomorrow, she was wasting her energy scraping with pieces of toilet paper. Empty the wastepaper basket, overflowing with junk. She carried it to the large bin in the kitchen. Papers, crumpled tissues, razor blades fell out, followed by a heap of reddish brown stuff. Francesca gasped and stood back. Feeling sick, she gazed incredulously down at so much hair. It must have been down to M's waist! She did not want to touch it, but could see it was good hair, rich, thick, and glossy, perhaps the one feature which had saved M's homeliness. What had possessed her to throw it away? Was it anything to do with the smashing of all the dishes? These things seemed awfully extreme measures to take, just to keep yourself from looking in the mirror.

She remembered that story about Van Gogh's ear and wondered if artists and idealists had larger capacities for such mortifications.

15 AMANUENSIS

"How did you spend your evening?" asked M.

"My evening?" Francesca had just arrived for work Wednesday morning, dressed for floor scrubbing. She had stopped off at the supermarket again and bought cloths, sponges, and the floor wax Cameron used. "I went back to the hotel and thought about going out to dinner. But I don't like to eat alone. I fell asleep instead. How was your evening?"

"Worked like a fiend. I can't tell you what a relief it

is to have those . . ." M brushed her hands away from her, as though warding off something unpleasant ". . . other things taken care of. Thank you for the kitchen window. You really are assisting me in becoming transparent."

"I'm going to do the floor now," said Francesca. "And then I thought I'd put some of those books back on the shelves. There are a lot overdue from a library, you know. Oh, and when I was hanging up some clothes and things, I found your checkbook. So maybe we could take care of some of the bills you mentioned." She did not mention her own thirty dollars. Surely M would think of that herself.

"Oh!" M clutched herself and bowed her shaved head upon her typewriter.

"What's wrong?" Francesca wondered if an amanuensis must be a nurse as well.

"The mere mention of . . . that sort of thing . . . destroys my equanimity. Now I won't be able to work." She piled her arms in their loose black sleeves over her head. Francesca was reminded of an old-fashioned photographer going beneath his curtain.

"I'm sorry. I shouldn't have mentioned it. Maybe you would like some coffee. I bought some instant yesterday."

"There's no tea, is there?" The head poked up slightly beneath the black sleeves.

"I could go out and get some."

"Never mind. There's nothing I like better than a cup of good green tea, however. Fix us both a cup of coffee and then come and talk to me until I get my transparency back."

When Francesca returned with the two cups, M said,

scrutinizing her curiously, "Tell me, what sort of thoughts does a person like you have when she's by herself?"

Francesca sat down. She sipped the coffee. It was awful. She had used too much, she guessed. She was not sure exactly what kind of person a person like herself was. M did not seem to notice how bad the coffee was. "I just ramble mentally, I guess," said Francesca.

"What sort of ramblings are they? Do you daydream, do you worry about the future? Are you aware of all the unforeseen catastrophes that may be lurking in your future?"

"Oh, I daydream. I worry. I don't think too much about catastrophes. I think it's better to take those things as they come." Francesca could tell from the look on M's face that she was being disappointing. She tried to think of something interesting. "There is this woman next door to me in the hotel," she said, "who cries all the time and is sick in the bathroom. For two nights, I've heard her. She talks over the phone and cries, and then she goes into the bathroom and has diarrhea. Last night, just before I fell asleep, I thought I heard her praying in German. Maybe she has just come to this country and doesn't know anyone. I have imagined some catastrophes about her. Like, what if she should commit suicide? What if her loneliness should become unbearable? And there is this other woman, the maid was telling me about her . . ."

M looked over her typewriter at Francesca. "What about you? Aren't you alone? What if your loneliness becomes unbearable? Haven't you imagined just how bad it might get?"

"I try not to imagine too far ahead," said Francesca,

frowning. "I told you, I was depressed when I couldn't find a job and when Nina Brett said I was a bad risk." What did this woman want from her?

"Well what did you do in this moment of depression? How did you act?"

Francesca thought back. She was not enjoying this conversation. She thought it would be of more use to them both if she went and scrubbed the floor. M seemed to be trying to unravel her, but maybe it was for the purposes of the Project. "I went downstairs and had some breakfast. Then this ex-priest sat down and I talked to him. Then I went back up to my room . . . no, I stopped into a perfume shop on the way . . . then went up to my room and waited for the maid to finish. Then I lay down on the bed for awhile. And then . . . well, then I remembered your ad, I had jotted your number down on a piece of paper, and I called you."

"What did you think when you were lying down?"

"I can't remember. Maybe I wasn't thinking anything. Maybe I was just waiting for something to happen. And it did."

M pondered. "Perhaps there are some people to whom things just happen, and other people who have to make things happen for themselves. I think I can work now. Run along and do your floor and I'll see you later."

Relieved, Francesca went off to the kitchen. It was the brightest room in the house, since she had cleaned the window. She opened the window, as the room still retained some of yesterday's odors. She scrubbed the floor with one of the new sponges. The effect was not very successful. The dirt was deeply ingrained and the floor should probably have been scraped first. She scrubbed it a second time, occasionally sitting back on her heels to get her breath, it was so hot, and trying to catch herself in the act of thinking something, in case M were to quiz her later on what she thought while scrubbing the kitchen floor. To her dismay, her thoughts kept being critical ones about M. She did not want to repeat them, especially to M. What did she know about artists and idealists, anyway? Not much. She waxed the floor and stood at the edge of the kitchen, not having much faith in that magic moment when the floor would suddenly begin to shine, like Cameron's did. The magic moment did not come. The wax dried into a dull yellowish film, beneath which the deep dirt still showed. Francesca sighed.

She tiptoed back to the front room where M was typing. She picked up some of the books and one or two pieces of broken china.

M stopped typing and pulled out a sheet of paper. "Read this and tell me what you think."

Francesca took the paper, closely typed from top to bottom, with hardly any margin. The top part began: NOTES FOR A YOUNG WOMAN. She scanned it quickly and blushed. All of her own physical features, some of the very sentences she had just finished saying, not a half hour ago. Then there was a summing up: "Extraordinarily beautiful, but never really contemplates the POWER a beautiful person can wield. Can be hurt, weep, suffer, but suffering passes quickly over her like summer storm. Not given to self-reflection or deep insights into others. Though feels the problems of others to be more interesting than her own. Generous but naive."

The second part of the page seemed to be a continuation of some earlier notes on A CHARISMATIC PERSON . . . "of enormous energies, uncertain identity and obscure origins . . . avoids all public occasions . . . living and working at own pace, paying no attention to fashions, tendencies, contingent realities, the worthless opinions of others . . . close-mouthed about own private life, self-effacing to the point of anonymity . . . is NEVER photographed, refuses to answer the telephone except for emergencies, sends back letters of a personal nature with 'addressee unknown' marked on them . . . this person's private life is a chain of mysteries, but the work done by this person a force recognized by all as significant . . ."

"Just the top part, don't read that other," said M. "Well, what do you think?"

"What is it for?"

"Just maybe it's a brief preliminary sketch of a person I want to add to my Desirable World," said M slowly, looking Francesca intensely in the eye.

Francesca handed back the paper. She did not look at M. She was trying not to think suspicious, unfair thoughts, but it gave her the creeps. What if M's Desirable World spilled off the paper and into this room? She had a horrible image of M suddenly jumping up from her table and running over and enveloping her in that black muu-muu.

"So, what are your impressions?" persisted M.

"I wonder what makes people want to re-create the world, make a better one," said Francesca. "My husband, for example. He seems to have a blueprint too."

"What is it like? What are its features?"

"I don't know. It's not a thing he discusses. It's just a thing I infer from his words and actions. I know he carries a sort of model world around inside his head. He's always comparing things to it. It's as if there's a perfect one of everything in his world and he keeps checking the real things against his own private ones. For instance, I think there's a perfect me inside his head and I often catch him looking or listening to me and comparing me with her . . ." she paused. She had not known she thought this till she said it now. That was why it was helpful to have a woman to talk to, a woman like the old Kate, a woman—give or take the creepiness—like M.

"Your husband sounds interesting. Is he a good man?" asked M.

"He's . . . very good at . . . everything he does. He has very high ideals, very high expectations of himself and others . . ."

M was nodding.

"He's not an extremely warm person and sometimes he can be awfully critical . . . but yes, I think he is probably a good man. He likes to take care of things, people."

"Then why are you leaving him?"

"Because he . . . because he paralyzes me."

"Paralyzes you *how*? With admiration or boredom or repulsion or what? There are many types of paralysis."

"I feel I'm useless, both to myself and him. There is nothing I can do for him that he can't do better for himself."

"Ha!" snorted M, "he can't cling to his own arm and enter rooms enhancing himself with your beauty."

"Oh beauty," said Francesca, wishing they would not go back to that.

"Don't sneer at what you've never had to do without," said M. "The un-beautiful are the unacknowledged minority group of this world. Beauty can get you a lot of things, my dear."

"Not everything," said Francesca, thinking of Mike. She missed him terribly at just this moment. The reason I am sitting here in this hot, messy apartment letting a bald woman who may or may not be insane pry into my personal life is because of Mike, she thought. The discrepancy between his remembered caresses, their easy, loving impersonality, and the cold, too-personal scrutiny of this woman was too much. She said, "If you'll tell me where the correspondence is, I think I'll start on that."

"Oh all right, then," sighed M. She began pulling envelopes out of drawers, her sighs becoming louder and wearier. "Oh shit, my subscription to *Vogue*'s run out." She glared at a card. "And the blasted electricity bill . . . '*Dear* Customer, have you forgotten something?' They have you, they have you every time. All efforts of transcendence of the body, of anonymity are ultimately grounded by these petty intrusions . . . no matter how one tries to efface oneself, she still has to see out of her goddam eyes and you sure as hell can't do that without light . . . I wonder what the saints did . . . they had candles, of course, which their monasteries paid for. Oh, I'm getting in a foul humor. I won't be able to go on." Down went the bald head on the typewriter. Up went the black curtain of sleeves.

"Never mind," said Francesca. "I'll see how far I can get on my own. If there's something I can't handle, I'll come and ask you."

"I'm sure you'll do fine!" murmured M beneath the sleeves. "Just use your imagination."

Francesca took the mail and went back to the kitchen, which was the cleanest spot in the apartment. She spread out the envelopes on the floor and sat down and surveyed them. *Thelma Postgate.* So that was what M was called before her "death." She had to admit, M Evans was neater, more charismatic.

She opened the bills. In the other room, M began typing again. Thelma Postgate was overdue on everything. Nasty letter from a real estate agency. Two months overdue on rent. Gas. Electricity. Phone! Francesca looked at two pages of calls, calls to everywhere, ranging from $1.65 to Chicago to $3.25 to Albany to $54.00 to Liverpool. The total bill came to $115.11. Most of the calls had been made on a single date in July, about three weeks ago. There were notices galore on overdue library books. Second notices, third notices. On one, a third notice for a book called Raglan's *The Hero,* a note was scrawled: "Please! Another person wants this book!" There was a printed reminder from a dentist, with Thelma's name written in by hand:

Thelma:

It is our office policy to notify patients on record for periodical examinations of the mouth. May I suggest you make appointment(s) for the following service(s):

The box labeled "continuation of incompleted treatment" had been checked and a further personal scribble added which said, "Do let us finish those gum treatments!" Francesca put this reminder to one side. Whatever else M did toward self-effacement, she really should not let her teeth go.

Then Francesca concentrated on the personal correspondence, considerably leaner than the bills.

Dear Thelma

Sorry if I sounded brusque when you telephoned last Thurs., but to tell the truth I was completely caught off guard, not having heard from you since college. Also Jay and I were having a small dinner party. I am so sorry to hear you're in a low period. Can you come to us in Saunderstown and stay a while? We'd adore having you, that is, if you can bear the children's* noise, and you know how hectically I live. Jay says he'd be interested in meeting my old roommate, and . . . but I'll close now and get this off quickly, so I can have your answer soon.

Love,
Phyllis

* Four of them! Has it been that long since we were gay irresponsible girls?

Thel,

You were so upset when I left that I called soon after from a nearby pay phone, but you'd either gone out or weren't answering. I didn't come back because we would just have started again. I wish I could have made you understand that it had NOTHING TO DO with any "lack" in you. If anywhere, the lack is in myself. I have so many problems of my own, I just could not rise to your rather special, unconventional needs.

But that is no reason to berate yourself, you are made of finer stuff. Not many of us have progressed as far as you in sloughing off old traditions, old demands, and specifying a Desirable World, and you mustn't feel a failure (neither should you be too hard on us) when the occasional interloper like myself stumbles into your World, can't find a place to sit down, and stumbles sadly out again. I do hope I helped some. And I am sure you'll find someone to take my place.

Affectionately,
V.

Both letters were postmarked approximately three weeks ago. The third, and last, was typed on the law firm stationery of Harrison T. Postgate of Albany.

Dearest Thelma:

I am sorry the reduced amount of your last quarterly check from Banker's Trust distressed you so, but the securest of legacies fluctuates with the market these days. Try and make do with the realities, my dear, we all have to. Most young women, after all, must resort to gainful employment or marriage, not being fortunate enough to have independent incomes. No one I know of lives "totally unencumbered by demeaning contingencies." (By the way, I should look up that word again, if I were you, I think you have it confused with "necessities.") Nor can I agree with you that it is a state to be actively striven for. To my knowledge, it has been achieved only by the dead.

Your Loving Uncle Harry

P.S. *As you know, I like to make Christmas plans well in advance. Any prospect of seeing you in Albany? If not, I shall probably go back to Tunis for a bit of digging.*

Francesca went back to the bills. She consulted the hardly legible balance in M's checkbook. $302.29. Could that be right? That wouldn't even cover the rent that was due. How had M gotten herself into these straits? She looked at some of the entries in M's check register, but they were either illegible or to individual names like "Mac-Ginn . . . Doug Arnold . . . C. Lane." Some were for very large amounts, up to $750. Francesca did not see how she was going to be of help without knowing more of the facts of M's life. Yet she shuddered at the thought of what these facts might be. There were several checks for small amounts, five dollars, seven dollars, made out to "V." Was that the "V" of the farewell letter? Was "V" a man or a woman? Had "V" been M's last amanuensis? What were the "rather special, unconventional needs" this "V" had alluded to? How was she going to pay these bills? M said to use her imagination, but she would need more than that. Francesca suddenly remembered that a large check awaited her in this very city, the bank draft Cameron had promised to send for the clothes. Perhaps she might help M out a little, just till she got on her feet . . . Then she remembered the last words of M's NOTES FOR A YOUNG WOMAN: *generous but naive.*

Resolutely, she got up from the floor and went to consult M, bracing herself against another explosion over contingencies. M had stopped typing and was leafing contentedly through an art book.

"Excuse me, M, I have to ask you . . ."

M looked up and beamed, showing the prominent gap-teeth. Francesca mentally restored M's hair and tried to visualize how she had looked before that day three weeks ago. An awful lot of things must have happened three weeks ago. Had they been catastrophes or contingencies?

"These letters from your uncle . . . and V . . . and Phyllis. How should I answer them? And is this the right balance in your checkbook?"

M condescended to glance briefly at the figure. "Goodness. I don't know. I think there is probably more than that." She shrugged and smiled appealingly up at her amanuensis. "What you obviously should do is pay a little bit to this one and a little bit to that one. A bit here, a bit there. Just keep the wolf from the door. And, regarding those . . . other letters, well, what could be simpler? The person to whom those letters are addressed is dead. Is that all?"

Francesca murmured yes and started back to the kitchen.

"Except for the uncle, of course!" M called after her. "He, unfortunately, remains a minimal contingency."

Francesca sat down on the floor and wrote out a check for one month's rent. She wrote out a check for the gas and electricity. She paid forty dollars down on the phone bill. She renewed the subscription to *Vogue,* checking the box marked "Bill me later." She figured M needed the subscription for her research on beautiful people.

She returned to search for paper and envelopes on M's table.

"Come here a minute," said M, motioning Francesca close to her side. She pointed to a picture in the art book. "What do you think of him?"

Francesca bent down to look at the picture. M's breath was close to her ear. Francesca knew M was looking at the side of her face and not down at the book.

She tried to concentrate on a pretty young man with a faraway look wearing a leather cuirass and shoulder armor. He held a sword in his right hand and the head of a snake in his left. He was barelegged and wore soft shoes that laced up his ankles. Coiled in a heap beneath his feet was the rest of the snake.

"Don't you think he is a little insipid looking? Tell the truth. I always want your honest judgment in these matters."

"Who is he?"

"The Archangel Michael, victorious over the Devil. I am coming to a startling conclusion in my research, Francesca. I am coming to the conclusion that strong men, heroes, extraordinary and powerful people are often portrayed with insipid, prissy features. In my World, I think I am going to give the good men the faces of villains."

"Won't that confuse everybody?"

"Oh everybody!" snorted M. "I can't worry about everybody! I have to get the place right for myself first."

"May I have some paper and envelopes?"

"No envelopes, sorry. Never use 'em. Here's some paper. Don't you have envelopes free at your hotel?"

"Oh. Yes."

"Well, you can mail everything off in your hotel envelopes," said M brightly. Francesca decided not to remind M of the matter of postage.

"Would you please sign these checks?"

"Certainly!" Magnanimously M scribbled the name of the deceased Thelma Postgate on the checks Francesca

had made out in her neat printing. She did not so much
as glance at the amounts.

"Thank you."

"Don't mention it. Francesca, I think I am going to become very fond of you. 'She walks in beauty . . .' Do you
know that poem? There is something enormously reassur-
ing about having a person like yourself moving softly,
efficiently about the premises."

"Thank you." Francesca went back to the kitchen. She
would finish these letters and clear up a bit more and
leave early. Perhaps take those books back to the library.
Just drop them in a slot outside, have the taxi stop and
drop them in. At least the fines would stop accumulating.

She sat down on the floor and began to write answers to
the letters. Her throat felt scratchy and she was beginning
to get a headache.

Dearest Uncle Harry, (she wrote)
 *Thank you for your kind invitation for Christmas but I will
be unable to make it to Albany. I hope you have a good time in
Tunis. Thank you for your advice, also.*
                                            Your Loving Niece

"Excuse me, shouldn't you sign this letter to your uncle?"
she called.

"Sign it yourself! He won't know the difference!"

Francesca signed "Thelma," folded the letter, and put it
in her purse. She would have to buy a plain envelope. It
would not do to use her hotel ones on Uncle Harry.

She re-read the other two letters. Then she found she

could re-seal them, more or less successfully. She wrote "addressee unknown" on them and put them in her purse along with the signed checks and the letter to Uncle Harry.

16 FREE WOMAN

"BEAUTY in our time . . ."
It was Thursday evening. Francesca had been in her hotel room since five thirty. She had chills and her stomach felt funny. She was waiting for Mike's promised call, reasoning to herself that the chills and the nervous stomach might be in anticipation of this call. She was leafing for the third time through a fashion magazine which she had bought after leaving M's. She had done very little work today. M had not seemed to mind. "Sit down and talk to

me. You've probably overdone yourself. What was it like, growing up in that town?" M had wanted to know all about Francesca's childhood, her relationship with Kate, their travels, what sort of advice Kate had given her about dealing with men, Kate's marriage to Francesca's father, Kate's marriage to Jonathan, and Kate's marriage to Ware. M took particular relish in this last relationship, probing Francesca to remember everything. M said thoughtfully, "People commit thousands of small suicides every day that go unnoticed."

Francesca had studied all the fashions in this magazine ad nauseam. She had read part of a feature with photographs on Mr. and Mrs. (Somebody Important's) penthouse apartment in this city. ("Although Mrs.——— dismisses her role in her husband's demanding life by saying simply 'He runs his office, I run his home,' she, too, is concerned with the world outside . . .") Now she was reading an essay entitled "The NOW Beauty." But her attention was divided between it and other things: Mike's call, her body's uneasiness, and the woman in 313.

The next door weeping had begun, punctuated by the trips to the bathroom. Francesca was seriously debating with herself whether or not it was her duty to knock on this fellow human being's door and ask if she could be of help. But there were problems. Which door should she knock on? If she left her room and went down the hall to knock, she might not be able to reach her phone on the first ring and Mike would hang up. And yet, it seemed somehow ungraceful to knock on the bathroom door when the woman was in there. Also the woman might resent her interference. Perhaps she preferred to suffer alone. She had not made the phone calls tonight, but simply kept up a steady, soft sobbing interrupted by an occasional cry that sounded like "God!" or "Gott!"

Francesca thought about women in rooms alone, weeping, waiting. She thought of the old lady upstairs who did not know how to turn on a stove. She would have to remember this, to tell M on Monday, "Thursday night I was thinking in my room . . ." When Francesca had confessed to M this afternoon that she thought she might have a fever, M had sent her away at once. "Stay in bed tomorrow, rest, don't come back till Monday. You may be getting the flu or something. I certainly hope I don't get it. Flu would set me back for days in my work." Francesca fought down the thought: M is a very selfish person. Artists of the Ideal *were* selfish perhaps . . .

Until very recently, she read in the magazine, *man was in the judgment seat of Paris, weighing and deciding what was most valuable in woman . . .*

What if he forgot to call? Never intended to call? On the other hand, it was entirely possible that she would be with him at this time tomorrow. Entirely possible! What had he said, his exact words? ("I might even arrange it so I can get back for the weekend. Would you be free if I could arrange it, Francesca?") She had hoarded these words for four days, keeping them a secret even from herself to pacify the fates.

She was free from now until Monday. "Go home and rest," said M, "you have exhausted me with all this talk. Take a long weekend, dear, you've earned it! Stay in bed tomorrow, rest . . ." She had said nothing about Francesa's having earned any money. "Did you mail those bills?" she had asked this morning. Francesca said she had. "And I wrote your uncle a polite note declining Christmas in Albany." "Good. Thelma never spent Christmas in Albany in her life. It is an empty form he must go through every July. And what about those other letters, what did you do with them?" "Well, I wrote 'addressee unknown' on the envelopes and sent them back." "Wonderful idea!" cried M. "What a clever amanuensis you are!" "It was your idea," said Francesca. "I got it from your NOTES ON A CHARISMATIC PERSON." "Ah, of course!" M had beamed. "Life after death keeps one so busy she can't keep track of her own inventions."

But the new woman, Francesca read in the magazine, *has gained enough assurance to judge what is most valuable in herself . . . Is beautiful because she is bold in affirming her existence as a free being . . . Has ceased being the 'Warrior's Delight' and has become the proud and equal fighter in the noble war of Life and Love . . .*

"*Gott!*" came the cry through the walls.

M puzzled Francesca, made her a little sad. M was not yet at home in her transparent self, she was still clouded and colored with petty moods, egocentricities which betrayed her high intentions. Francesca worried how desirable M's Desirable World would be when it was finished. Could a thing be better than the person who made it? She wondered what Cameron would think of M. They were both idealists. She was pretty sure he would dismiss M as a freak. Yes, M would seem ridiculous to Cameron.

The phone rang and it was Mike.

"How are you?" he asked. They had a bad connection. She could hear another conversation going on in the interstices of their own. Two men, talking and laughing.

"I got a job."

"That's wonderful! You see, I told you you could do it." Pause. Francesca heard one of the men laugh. *Oh yeah, did he really?* he said.

"I thought you might not call." Now why had she gone and said that.

"I said I would. I've thought of you a lot, Francesca."

"Oh Mike. Will I see you this weekend? I've got to-morrow off from my job. The whole weekend free."

"I can't make it this weekend, honey."

What was that? Did he say I *can* or I *can't?* Those other voices! Shut up! One of them said, *Not bad for a guy his age.* They went off into gales of laughter. "I can't *hear* you, Mike."

"I can't make it, Francesca. I'll try very hard to come the weekend after. Can you hold out for me that long, or have you found somebody else already?" His voice was light, teasing. She did not like it.

"There's *nobody* else. Oh, Mike, I wish . . ." Out of the past came a piece of the old Kate's lore to stifle her. *Never push a man. Never beg or wheedle or make them feel guilty. Men hate that.*

"I know you're disappointed, honey."

"Yes. I'm disappointed. But . . . I understand." An awful thing was happening. Deep down in her bowels, every-thing was letting go. She sat up straighter on the bed, gripping her legs together and holding herself in.

"Good girl. I really have missed you, you know. That's such good news about the job. What kind of job is it?"

"Oh, it's . . . I'm a sort of private secretary to this woman.

This—writer." The job suddenly meant nothing. It was absurd. It was not even a real job. Francesca felt she had cheated herself, gotten tangled up with some lonely lesbian on the ninth floor of a shabby building, scrubbed her floor, had a few typically female conversations, and nothing real to show for it. *She had to go to the bathroom . . .*

"A writer. How exciting. I had no idea you'd find something so interesting. What kind of things does she write? Is any of it published?"

"I don't think so. I think her work is still in the planning stages." *I'll see you then. Tell Martha we'll be in Toronto around the twelfth,* said one of the voices. *Good enough, Ralph, see you then!* Click. A faint dial tone. Francesca had Mike all to herself. Tears of discomfort slid down her face and into the little holes of the mouthpiece. She *had* to go to the bathroom . . .

"I see," said Mike. "Well. It still sounds fascinating. And it's something to keep you busy."

"Mike, I wonder—could you possibly call me back?"

"Call you back? What's the matter, don't you want to talk to me any more? Got a heavy date?"

"No. No! That's not it. Could you call me back in ten minutes?"

"Gosh, Francesca, I can't, I'm afraid. The thing is, I'm between places right now. I'm on my way somewhere and I'm already late. Tell you what. I'll call you sometime this weekend, Saturday afternoon, Sunday afternoon? But don't wait inside all day or anything like that. I'll keep trying. And we'll see what's new then. How is the old hotel, holding up all right?"

"It's all right. Look Mike, I have to go . . ." She almost sobbed. What a traitor the body was!

"I get the message. Be in touch with you soon. Bye, honey."

She slammed down the receiver and rushed for the bathroom. There was still an odor from the other woman's sickness. She put her face down in her hands and retched. The tears soaked through her fingers. Everything so ugly, so sickening, so cheap. And on top of that, her body was coming apart, it seemed to be turning to water. *Perhaps I am getting some kind of virus.* Everything was turning to water and running out of her. She had no real job, no real lover. Both were imitations, would not hold up under crises. How could he have thought she had another lover . . . a "heavy date" . . . and she had been fantasizing *marrying* him. She put her head down on her knees, giving herself up entirely to her sickness. How apt it seemed, how fit. She wept.

There was a soft knock on the bathroom door. "*Bitte . . .*" said a woman's voice, "*Bitte . . .*" Then a question. Francesca did not know the language but she understood.

"Thank you. I am all right. Thank you."

The other murmured something. Francesca heard her move away from the door, the feet on the carpet. It was probably exactly like her own room in there, only everything in reverse, mirror image. She heard the sigh of springs as the woman sank down on her bed.

Francesca returned to her own bed. She was shivering a great deal. She got under the covers with her clothes on. She picked up the magazine. Hadn't she been in the middle of something? Yes . . .

*The new woman is triumphant, a young warrior . . . Man
confronted with her mobility, her energy, her drive toward her own unique destiny, has had to alter his concept
of feminine beauty . . . In her exciting transformation she
carries him with her to a higher plane of evolution, a realm
where there are no petty border skirmishes between the
sexes, but a realm of partnership, freedom, equality, faith,
love. This is the realm of true beauty . . . beauty NOW.*

On the facing page was a woman whose hair had been
dyed a pale gold and cut short and close to her head like
a helmet. She wore gold armor in which jewels were set,
and her eyeshadow was also gold. Her face was very pale,
very aloof, a little like Nina Brett's. Her eyes gazed raptly
ahead, focused on some triumph Francesca could not see.

The bed was so cold. Francesca called out, "Kate, could
you bring me a blanket please?" Kate came into the dark
room. She stood in the doorway, a beautiful glittering ap-
parition, dressed to go out, a blanket in her arms. "I'm
freezing, Kate." Kate covered Francesca's shivering body.
Outside the window were millions of stars. They seemed
to be sending cold blasts of air down through the night,
breathing their icy separate breaths on Francesca's body.
"I'm so cold." "We are going to that silly New Year's
Party," said Kate, her voice cool and brittle as the stars.
Now the form of a man stood in the doorway. He wore
evening clothes. "Are those new earrings, Kate? Those
diamonds in your ears?" "No, they are made of ice.
Aren't they lovely? Your father gave them to me . . ."

Why is it so cold in here?

❀   ❀   ❀

Francesca, linked to her father's arm, walked through a luxuriant, tropical park. Exotic birds fluttered down and up again, uttering wild cries. Her father had become younger since his death and affected a dandyish mode of dress, very unlike his former style. They had been speaking about Francesca's education, though she could remember nothing of what had been said. Now her father pursed his lips and said in a precise voice, "Your mother, I am sorry to say, is showing her age. If only she had listened to me, we could have stopped it! Do you know Madam? She has a little concession just the other side of the park. Perhaps it is not too late."

Madam's house appeared, a hut with trees around it. The trees had feathers instead of leaves. An ugly old woman sat behind a table with a dirty cloth on it. The crystal ball on the table was filthy. There were pots and jars of greasy-looking creams, eyeshadows, all colors of makeup.

"Madam, this is my beloved daughter," said Francesca's father.

"Sit down," said Madam with a heavy accent. "What experience have you had?"

Behind Madam, on a shelf, were huge apothecary jars filled with beauty potions in wild colors.

"I've worked a little . . ." Francesca began.

"Quiet!" cried her father. "Do you want to ruin your chances? Do you want to resort to gainful employment?"

The beauty potions in the apothecary jars bubbled and moved, swirls of color coming alive.

"So many things are changing . . ." Francesca's father said conversationally to Madam. "I make my Christmas plans further and further ahead each year."

The hag winked at Francesca. She unstoppered one of the apothecary jars, dabbed her fingers in the bubbling stuff, and touched Francesca's father's face, leaving a greenish streak.

"I'm sorry, you don't understand," he said. "It's not for me, it's for my wife . . ."

Francesca watched, horrified, as the green streak slowly spread down the side of her father's face, coiled around his neck, became a snake and choked him to death.

"Now, darling," said the hag. She dipped her fingers into another jar, a sort of peachy-gold.

"No, please." Francesca was paralyzed.

"I only want to kiss you," said the hag, her fingers dripping with cream. She came closer, turning into a beautiful young man.

Francesca closed her eyes. She felt her body beginning to dissolve, slowly, slowly, naturally, as if she were a candle thrust into a fire and held there. Then suddenly she wanted the feeling. "Melt me, oh please melt me," she cried. "Melt me down till I am unrecognizable . . ."

Warm, at last. Dissolved in such warmth.

17   CONSERVATOR

Toward morning, Francesca got up and vomited, took off
her clothes, turned out the light, and got back to bed just
before fainting. As she lost consciousness she saw Cameron's face. Floating sternly in the void, it commanded her
focus until she passed out.

She was wakened by a maid, not the friend of the day
before. "Sorry, I thought you'd gone. It's two o'clock. Do
you want any towels?"

"Just leave them on the chair."

"Are you sick?"

"I'm all right now. I had an upset stomach."

"Okay." The woman left.

Francesca turned her face to the wall. She was too weak to move, to think. She curled herself tight under the bedclothes and closed her eyes and drifted. She had no will to resist. Voices chatted with her, lectured her, admonished her, questioned her. She added up figures, multiplied them, divided, subtracted them. She made out checks. She heard deep booming, like the ocean, then alarm bells, ringing, ringing, warning . . . she realized the telephone was ringing. Perhaps now that she was too sick to care, Mike would come after all.

"Hello . . ."

"Francesca?"

"Cameron!"

"You didn't call last night. You promised."

"Last night?" What was last night? Had she promised? If he said so, she must have promised. "I'm sorry. I'm sick. If only you were here!"

"I am here. I'm downstairs in the lobby of your hotel."

Cameron made Francesca's bed with her still in it. He plumped up her pillows, criticizing their skimpiness. He bathed her face and arms with a damp cloth. He called room service and ordered orange juice and dry toast.

"I want that freshly squeezed, please. I see. Well, ask the boy to go out and get some. My wife is ill. I'll see that he's taken care of."

He went through her closet and checked her clothes. He said very little. He looked older and thinner. There was a dark puffiness beneath his eyes. She felt sorry for him and ashamed that she had caused him to sit up all night on an airplane. She wept a little, for what reason she couldn't say. She wept with relief and with sadness. Cameron bathed her face some more and told her not to cry in front of the room-service boy when he came.

After she had her juice and toast, she drifted again. She was aware of Cameron opening the curtains, worrying the air-conditioner till he found a quieter frequency, sitting in the mustard-colored chair and leafing through her fashion magazine. She heard him tear something out.

He came and stood by her bed. "I'm going out for a while. Will you be all right?"

"Where are you going?"

"To take care of some things. I'll be back soon. You're going to be better tomorrow."

She lay alone in the softly darkening room. The mustard chair bore the imprint of his afternoon watch. The room was changed, it no longer seemed capable of holding any-one's solitude. She lay and waited for him to come back.

He returned with fruit: apples, pears, and the black grapes she loved best, the ones that had sweet skins and were tart on the inside. He called room service again.

"Yes. Please send up a large pot of hot water, two cups and saucers, two small plates, and some silverware. No, that's all. Oh for heaven's sake. I don't *want* anything from the kitchen. My wife is ill and I am going to make her some tea. So please send what I asked. I will take care of it."

He had brought back a tin of her favorite tea and a slim box of French soaps shaped like rosebuds. He washed her hands, with it, doing each of her fingers as one washes the hands of a child. He smelled her fingers. "Nice," he said. She, too, sniffed them. It was an agreeable smell, fresh roses.

After they had had their tea (which Cameron made) and fruit (which Cameron peeled) he said, "How are you feeling now?"

"Still a little weak. But better. Do you think I had a virus or intestinal flu or something? Maybe that's what the woman in 313 had. Only she's been sick since Monday."

Cameron gave Francesca an odd look and did not reply. He peeled himself a grape, deposited the skin on the side of his plate, and munched the grape reflectively. He had pulled the chair close to the bed and they were sharing Francesca's tray as a makeshift table. "What are your plans for the future?" he asked.

"Oh Cameron—"

He held up one hand to stop her, while delicately spitting a grape seed into his other hand. He took his plate into his lap and sat back. He put the grape seed on this plate. "I didn't come here to interfere with your plans or force you back. I wouldn't *want* to force you back. I came because I was worried. I had that ominous letter from you . . ."

"*What* ominous letter?"

"The one about the lady with no screens on her windows."

"That wasn't ominous. I was just telling you the news—"

"I received this letter Thursday. Then I waited in vain for your promised Thursday evening call. I decided to come and see if you needed me. I'm not quite certain what you are up to. I see that you've bought no clothes and I find that you haven't cashed my bank draft. But as long as you know what you're doing, that's all right. I'm taking an afternoon plane home tomorrow. More tea? No? Anyway, I'm glad to see your appetite has improved." He poured himself another cup.

"Cameron, you don't really need me in your life."

"You're projecting again, Francesca. Perhaps what you mean to say is that you no longer need me."

"I do need you. No I don't. You're confusing me in that way you always do. Your words confuse things."

"I don't wish them to. I wish them to clarify things."

Francesca sank back on her pillows and groaned. "Oh, why did you marry me?"

He sighed. "Of course, what you're asking is: Why did you marry me. I have often asked myself that. I don't dwell on it, because I don't believe in questioning my good fortune too closely. So I can't answer the question you are really asking. I married you because you are the best for me."

"But why? Why am I? Is it because of the way I look, or because I was rude to you that first time, what? Please, Cameron, try and tell me. It's very important for me to know why I am valuable."

"You are valuable to *me*, Francesca, because you complete the shape of my life. I live in this shape, it defines me."

"Oh Cameron! What does that *mean*? You were already defined when you came to our house for dinner. You were defined years before. Jonathan told us about you. You were probably defined before you were born. I want to know why you wanted me!"

"You are going to think I'm being infuriatingly rhetorical, Francesca, but I have told you why you are valuable to me. If you want me to tell you why you should be valuable to yourself, I can't do that. Nobody can do that but you. I have often told you I want you to be your own woman. You underestimate my sincerity when I tell you that. But I assure you, I mean it."

"Well, what if I told you I had decided to be my own woman? What if I told you I had a job and intended to stay in this city and start a new life without you?"

"Are you telling me that now?"

"Yes. I think I am. No, I know I am. Cameron, I'm leaving you." She began to cry, but forced herself to look him in the eye.

He continued to sit back in his chair, one thin ankle crossed over the other knee, his fruit plate balanced in his lap. He watched her cry. He seemed to accept it as something natural, something that must be gone through. When she needed to blow her nose, he provided the handkerchief.

"I guess this will change everything for you," she said. "You'll have to find another shape and start all over again."

"No," he replied, rather dreamily. "No, nothing will change. Not for me." He got up and took her tray and began tidying things. He brushed the seeds and the peelings into a paper sack and put this sack into the wastebasket. He rinsed the cups in the bathroom. He seemed quite at home.

"What do you mean? How can it *not* change?"

He turned to face her. He stood poised on one foot, the other curled around his ankle. It was an odd, gawky, yet arrogant pose. Like a black heron. The gawkiness competed with the arrogance, and made this thin man in his dark clothes seem both foolish and fearsome.

"Some shapes can't be altered once they are made. The sacrament of marriage is such a shape. There are promises we make which bind us within their terrible spiritual force-field. You and I might live physically apart for the rest of our lives. And we will, if that's what you want. But we are eternally together in that spiritual field of force we created with our own vows."

Francesca pulled the covers up to her chin and stared at him. "You don't really believe that."

"I do believe it." He looked at his watch and slipped on his jacket.

"Where are you going?"

"For a walk."

"Are you coming back?"

"Do you want me to?"

"Yes. Just for a while. I don't want to be alone to hear that poor woman start crying in 313."

Cameron touched her forehead lightly with his fingers. "There is no woman in 313. I asked at the desk. From your description, I thought she might need help. 313 is empty."

Francesca looked into the flat gray-green eyes of her husband. "Maybe she checked out. She could have checked out today or yesterday."

"She could have," said Cameron. He went out.

18   PREPARATIONS FOR DEPARTURE

He sat in the chair, watching his wife sleep. The lamp burned above his head. Soon it would be Saturday morning outside the window. He had sat up all night for two nights. From time to time he would re-align his spine with the back of the chair, stretch his fingers and re-clasp them in his lap, cross the other ankle over the other knee. He would briefly close his eyes. Then he would open them and continue his vigil. He saw nothing but his wife.

She slept on her left side, her legs tucked up into the

curve of her body, making herself small. Her left arm was beneath the pillow. All that was visible of her face was the smooth forehead framed by a few damp wisps of hair and a flushed half-moon of cheek. Her right arm lay bare on top of the covers, the fingers curled a little inwards. He studied this arm, fascinated with its perfection. The upper part was firm and shapely, neither too plump nor too thin. It was an arm made for sleeveless dresses. It would look good for years to come. The color of the arm was a rich, ripe golden-pink. She had become quite tanned in the mountains, he had forgotten how wonderfully she tanned. The first time he had seen her, she had been this color, perhaps a little darker. She had been wearing a very light blue dress which left her arms and shoulders bare, which fastened in soft folds around her long neck, which moved silkily about her hips when she got up from the couch and went softly, coolly out of the room. Without a word to him, without even saying goodbye. He had waited for her to come back, spinning out trivial conversation with those others till he was bored out of his mind. She didn't come back. "Do say goodbye to your daughter," he had told the mother at the door. "That's her way," the mother had apologized. "She often gets sleepy and takes French leave."

Her forehead was completely smooth. Not a line. He often looked at the foreheads of women. The forehead of his secretary, for instance, had a set of deep horizontal ripples. She was always raising her eyebrows. It was her way of communicating. You could look at those ripples and you knew what kind of woman she was. The faces and foreheads of young women on the street: little apostrophies between the eyes, sharp little parentheses on either side of their determined mouths, all sorts of squiggles and ripples and jags indicating their struggle. He did not want his wife to struggle. He did not want a single sign of effort to leave its mark on that exquisite face.

The dawn was edging its way through the curtains. He stood up, turned off the lamp, squared his shoulders. He looked at his watch. He looked at his wife. Her mouth was slightly open and a tiny dewdrop of saliva had gathered at one corner. Her eyes moved faintly beneath the closed lids. A soft moan escaped. "Oh, Mike . . ." she said.

He wrote her a note: *Gone for a walk. Be back to say goodbye,* and slipped out of the room.

He went downstairs to the desk and paid her bill. He closed himself into a telephone booth and called his secretary in California. It was six a.m. there. Her husband answered and passed the receiver to her. They had both been asleep.

"Paula, I'm very sorry to wake you at this hour."

"Mr. Bolt? Is everything all right? Are you at home?"

"I'm in New York. I'll be coming back today. Paula, will you do me a favor? I'll make it up to you, for working on Saturday."

"Sure, Mr. Bolt. What?"

"I want you to go to a florist. Wait till late afternoon, so the flowers will be fresh. Buy roses. Lots of roses. All colors. Dozens and dozens. I want you to fill my apartment with roses."

"Oh, Mrs. Bolt must be coming with you."

"You have the key to my place. Now, you will have to

buy vases, too. The florist will probably have what you want. I want simple glass vases. Perhaps a few cut-glass. He'll be able to help you. I know I can count on you, Paula."

"Of course you can," replied his secretary.

After he had made this call, he walked to an airlines office. His ticket was soon ready. He tucked it into his breast pocket and returned to the hotel. He was tired. He stopped at the hotel coffee shop and ordered a cup of black coffee. While he was drinking it, he took out of his pocket a folded page from Francesca's fashion magazine. It was a full-color page of a beautiful woman, older than Francesca, modeling a very sheer orange dress, cut low, with many ruffles. The text at the bottom of this photograph read:

THE COUNTESS OF FORTRANNI models a dress from the new much-talked-about ST. AXEL collection, which can be seen currently at Bergdorf's. St. Axel says, "I believe we are rediscovering the form and elegance so absent from this modern era through the costumes of the past." His collection features dresses copied in complete detail from such Masters as Fra Angelico, Titian, Bronzino, Goya and Courbet. It includes a stunning reproduction from a Byzantine mosaic of the Virgin. "Costumes are psychological. Choose your costume, wear it, and one day you will become it," says this ingenious young designer, born Simon Ackelroyd 35 years ago in Paterson, N.J., who now lives in a thirteenth-century fortified castle on the Rhine. The Countess's dress: "I copied it exactly from a Pre-Raphaelite painting entitled *Flaming June*."

He refolded the page, replaced it in his pocket, and went up to his wife's room.

She was out of bed, had brushed her hair, and was sitting restlessly in the chair in her dressing gown. She had his note in her hand and looked troubled.

"You are better," he said. "You are looking splendid again."

"Am I? Yes, I am better. It seems to have disappeared, the virus, whatever I had."

"I've decided to take an early afternoon flight," he said. "It is going to be a busy weekend for me, and I don't want to interfere with yours."

"Oh, I'm not doing much of anything." She studied her fingernails.

"Then perhaps you would indulge me for the rest of the time I am here."

She looked at him.

"Will you let me take you shopping? I would like to buy you a coat."

"A coat? But it's August."

"Winter will come faster than you think. New York is not California. If you are going to stay in this city and be a working girl, you'll certainly need a coat."

"I suppose I will." She sounded uncertain.

He went to her closet and selected a dress. "Wear this," he said. "I like it best of all the ones you brought along."

"You're so funny sometimes," she said. She got up from the chair and came over to him and took the dress, stopping in front of the mirror to smooth her hair.

19 A COAT AND A DRESS

They took a taxi, although Francesca assured Cameron she felt well enough to walk. The virus or whatever it was had vanished as suddenly as it had arrived.

Outside the store, a blind man shuffled slowly along. He had a sign around his neck that said THERE BUT FOR THE GRACE OF GOD GO I. His dog followed, a mangy, sad animal that kept lying down. Cameron put some change into the blind man's cup, then held the door for his wife. Francesca went in the store, feeling proud of him.

"Go straight through," said Cameron, guiding her arm. "To the elevator. Not the least of this store's charms is that it refuses to put in an escalator."

They had the elevator to themselves. Cameron pressed a button. As they went up, Francesca began to feel more secure in herself. Shopping, trying on clothes, was one thing she could do as well as anyone in the world. It was one thing in which she could not be called inexperienced.

The elevator stopped, the doors opened, and Francesca and Cameron walked a short distance across thick carpeting to a desk. Behind this desk sat an immaculately attired young woman, wearing a suit and a hat with a sloping brim. She was impeccably made up, her face was a smooth, pleasant mask which betrayed nothing but the desire to be gracious. She reminded Francesca a little of Nina Brett —that is, if Nina Brett decided to be cheerful.

"Good morning," she said, her long-lashed, green-shadowed eyes sweeping appreciatively over Francesca, then up to Cameron. "May I help you?"

"Good morning," said Cameron. "Yes, thank you. My wife would like to see some coats."

"Certainly. Will you have a seat, please. I'll call someone." She motioned to a long velvet dais. Cameron and Francesca sat down, while she picked up a telephone.

"Miss Lurley? Can you show a lady and gentleman some coats?" she said into the receiver. "Wonderful." She hung up and turned to Cameron. "Miss Lurley is on her way." She wrote something down in a book.

"Thank you," said Cameron. He seemed at home.

Francesca looked around. Except for a discreet rack of suits, there were very few clothes on display here. The whole floor, full of soft furniture and alcoves and corners, looked like someone's living room. A silver-haired lady sat just within one of these alcoves, talking on the telephone. "Mrs. Healey's chauffeur is outside," she said. "Can you take the dress down? I'm afraid I can't. No, I have a fitting in three minutes. Good. Thank you." She hung up. Everyone so polite.

A dark-haired young woman marched out from behind a screen. She walked arrogantly, like a dancer, and wore a black dress with a high neckline and green-tinted glasses. "Good morning, Sir. Good morning, Madam. What sort of coat would you like to see?"

"Something workable, but warm," said Cameron.

Miss Lurley frowned. She looked them over, taking in their clothes.

"Fox, muskrat, perhaps a very good raccoon," said Cameron.

Miss Lurley smiled. "Will you come this way?" She led them behind the screen and down a carpeted corridor at the end of which hung a marvelous array of fur coats behind glass.

Miss Lurley opened the glass doors, stood pondering a moment, then selected a baby muskrat whose skins had been sewn together in a sportive, charming way. It had large lapels and a tie-around belt of fur. "Would you like to try it?" She held it for Francesca.

The yellow silk lining felt deliciously cool against her skin.

"Ah," said Cameron, as Francesca buttoned the coat, turned the collar up around her cheek and pretended to study the hemline in the mirror.

"What a lovely tan you have," said Miss Lurley. "Have you been to the beach?"

"My wife has been visiting her mother in the mountains," said Cameron. "How does the coat feel, Francesca? Raise your arms. Is there enough room beneath the arms?"

Francesca raised her arms and regarded her serious reflection. She saw their two admiring faces behind her, Cameron's and Miss Lurley's. They seemed to be in league together for her comfort, her pleasure.

"Beautiful," said Miss Lurley. "I'd say it's definitely the one. But we should try some more just to be sure."

"Yes," said Cameron, "just to be sure. Though, I agree. It seems right. How do you like the coat, Francesca?"

"Oh I like it. It will be . . . very warm," she said.

They made her try on a silver fox polo coat, an Icelandic dyed sheepskin which came to her ankles, a Spanish lamb, and a hefty Chinese raccoon.

"Oh dear!" cried Miss Lurley, sinking under the growing load of discarded furs, "I'd hate to be the one making the decision. All of them are made for her."

"I'm still partial to the little muskrat," said Cameron, smiling at Miss Lurley. "I'm inclined to think your first choice was intuitive."

"Perhaps it was," said Miss Lurley modestly.

"Francesca?"

Francesca loitered in front of the mirror, hugging the coat, the first coat, about her again. A lassitude had come over her, a sort of standing sleep within the coat. She felt she could go on standing here for hours, not really focusing on anything. She tried to imagine hurrying up

M's nine flights of stairs on a winter day, wearing this coat. It seemed absurd.

"I like it best, I think," she said. It didn't really matter.

"We'll take it," said Cameron to the other woman. "There's one more thing. I'm curious to see the St. Axel collection. Would you be able to show us that?"

"You know about the St. Axel," said Miss Lurley approvingly.

"I read something about it."

"Which ones were you interested in?" asked Miss Lurley. "You see, I'm afraid several of them are gone already."

"Oh, I hope the Byzantine mosaic isn't gone," said Cameron.

"The Madonna? No, it's still here. In fact, nobody has even tried it on that I know of. It's a formidable number."

"Why is that?"

"Well, for one thing, it's fairly heavy. There are seed pearls and semi-precious stones sewn into it. For another thing, very few women have the stature or the neck to get away with it. It has a very high neckline. In fact, I would say anything less than the tallest and most exquisitely boned woman would look ridiculous in it." Miss Lurley paused and let her eyes travel shrewdly over Francesca's face and neck and body.

"I want to see it," said Cameron. "Can you show it to us?"

"Certainly. Will you wait here? Please sit down and I'll run and fetch it. It's in another part of the store. I'll just take the muskrat along, shall I? They can be boxing it."

"Fine," said Cameron.

Miss Lurley went off, rather breathless, taking Francesca's new coat, and Cameron sat down on a bright green sofa. He motioned Francesca to sit beside him.

"Why do you want to see that dress?" she said. "What would I ever do with a dress with semi-precious stones all over it?"

"Indulge me a little longer." Cameron turned and gave her a deep, searching look. The intensity of it alarmed her. What did this new "indulgence" consist of?

Presently Miss Lurley returned, carrying something in a heavy plastic bag. She held it aloft by its hanger. She was accompanied by another woman, the silver-haired woman Francesca had overheard giving directions about Mrs. Healey's chauffeur.

"This is Mrs. Trinchieri," she told them. "Our floor manager."

Cameron stood up. "How do you do?" he said. "I am Mr. Bolt and this is my wife, Mrs. Bolt."

"How do you do?" said Mrs. Trinchieri. "You will excuse my coming along. This is somewhat of an event. The St. Axel collection has caused such a stir and I wanted to see someone model this particular number. It is so stunning. Miss Lurley said your wife," she nodded respectfully to Francesca, "was possibly the only woman she knew of who could dare try it on."

Cameron gave a slight bow.

"Will you come into the dressing room, Mrs. Bolt?" said Miss Lurley, leading the way to a pair of bright green curtains which matched the sofa. Francesca followed meekly. She felt as though she had been drawn into some sort of pageant, she was not sure at what moment it had begun. Mrs. Trinchieri stayed behind to chat with Cameron.

"If you'll take off your dress, I'll see if I can extricate this thing," said Miss Lurley. Now that the two women were alone, she had become more confidential, conspiratorial. "Will you look at the jewels on it?" She was pulling it heavily from the plastic bag. "What does your husband do?"

"He's District Attorney in California. He's . . . he may be the next Attorney General."

"I knew he was *something*," said Miss Lurley. She chewed her lower lip between her teeth as she unzipped the back of the dress.

Francesca shed her own dress and stood in bra and panties, her head lowered modestly on its long neck.

"I think the best way is for you to step in." Miss Lurley held the dress open for Francesca. "I can't get over that tan. It's such a warm, peachy color. Not *muddy* like some. You ought to be careful of your skin, though. Now, slip your arms in. The sleeves certainly do fit, don't they? I pity those poor women in ancient times, don't you? Buttoned up and down to the hilt. No wonder they were always fainting. You look—wait a minute, wait and let me zip you up. Hold tight, here we go. Oh my goodness. Wait till he sees this! Here, let me adjust those triple mirrors, and then we'll call the others in. You look otherworldly, don't you?" She flung back the green curtains. "Come and see, Mr. Bolt. Come and see this vision, Mrs. Trinchieri!"

They came.

"Oh!" said Mrs. Trinchieri, clasping her hands to her breast. She could not speak further, could only look with awe at the three madonnas in the triple mirror.

"She is like a vision, isn't she?" repeated Miss Lurley.

Cameron did not speak.

Francesca observed the little pageant in the triptych. She remembered how she and Kate had trooped dutifully through all those cathedrals in Europe. Scenes from her past life flashed before her, clothes she had tried on over the years, reflections of herself at six, at ten, at eighteen, at twenty, reflections in so many mirrors, all over the world.

"I think the skirt is a tad too long," ventured Mrs. Trinchieri at last. "It should touch the floor, but not drag it. Shall I pin it up, Mr. Bolt, just to see?"

"Would you do that?"

"I'll go and get my pins." Off she went.

"I wonder if you would excuse us a moment," said Cameron to Miss Lurley.

"Certainly. I'll be close by if you need me." And Miss Lurley, too, was gone.

"Cameron, you aren't thinking—"

"Yes, I think she's right. It's just that bit too long." Cameron knelt and turned up a portion of the hem between his fingers. "A half-inch will do it, no more."

Francesca gazed at the three Camerons kneeling at her feet. His head was bowed over the luxuriant folds of the costume. "I adore you in this," he said.

"But, Cameron—"

"I want it, Francesca." She couldn't see his face, just the top of his head, three heads, the mixture of reddish-brown and gray hair, three heads bowed.

"*You* want it?"

"I want to take it back with me. It will hang in your closet. I'll take it out sometimes and remember the morning you tried it on, when it touched your skin."

"Cameron, is this a joke?"

"It's not a joke," he said. He raised his head. Francesca stared, transfixed, into the triple mirror. She saw three Cameron Bolts with tears in their eyes.

20 THE BOLTS AT HOME

It was a Saturday morning in late October, and Francesca had just finished breakfasting in bed. Lately her appetite had increased and she consumed enormous breakfasts. Now she was drinking her tea in the sunshine that covered her bed, and examining two letters which had come for her in the morning's mail. The first she merely glanced at. She had expected it. The second was addressed in a bold, shapely hand. Francesca approved the heavy cream-colored notepaper. It was the kind she might have used herself. "Dear Mrs. Bolt . . ." it began and went on for two closely written sides of the page. It was signed Grace Fairfield, a name Francesca did not know.

Dear Mrs. Bolt,

My editor here at Chatelaine West *has asked me to approach you about the possibility of my doing a story on you for our spring number, which will be an issue devoted entirely to the wives of prominent men in politics, business and the arts.*

I am sure you shudder at the mere thought of being made the subject (or object!) of another one of those prepackaged confections which pass for personality profiles, in which Mrs. X, frozen by the photographer on a stiff chaise longue where she never ordinarily sits, lets the interviewer "draw" from her a favored recipe or two, a beauty secret, and perhaps one or two glowing allusions about her idyllic marriage to the Great Mr. X.

I have in mind something different. I would simply like to spend some time with you—as much as you have to spare— on several different occasions. I could visit you at your home, you could visit me at mine, maybe we could go to a film, an art gallery one afternoon. Just two women browsing and talking together, if you see what I mean.

I have had this urge to experiment within the particular limits of my kind of journalism for a long time. What gave me the courage to suggest this to you was that while researching your background, I discovered we were born on the same day of the same year! I found myself wondering what sort of person you were, how your life had differed from mine, what sort of things interested you, angered you, how you'd come to make the choices you did, comparing your life to mine. And I came up with my wild idea.

Would you be willing to try? I'm sending along, under separate cover, several recent issues of CW in which things of mine appear, just to show you that I can put decent sentences

together. But none of these pieces has the scope or the depth
I dare to think I can achieve with you.

I eagerly await your answer. Listed below are all my tele-
phone numbers and my home and office address.

Hopefully yours,
Grace Fairfield

Cameron came in to take her tray. He was dressed for
his Saturday golf game. She saw his eyes graze over her
letters, but he made no comment.

She handed him the letter from Grace Fairfield. "What
do you think I should do?"

Cameron sat down on the side of her bed with the letter.

"Mmm. It's certainly a *chatty* letter, isn't it?" He read
it to the end, raised his eyebrows, and handed it back to
Francesca.

"Well?"

"What do *you* think?" he asked. "Of course I wouldn't
mind seeing your picture on the glossy, thick pages of
Chatelaine West. I wonder who else they have in mind
for the issue."

"I'd kind of like to do it. She sounds like an interesting
person. Exactly my age." She laughed, "Who knows what
new things I might find out about myself."

"You'll find out exactly what you tell her. Interviewers
are like fortune tellers in that sense. I'm not trying to
discourage you from it, not at all, I'm just saying don't
expect any startling revelations about yourself."

"Oh, let me have faith in Grace Fairfield. It will give me
something to do. Cameron, will you win?"

"I haven't the slightest idea. Whether I win or don't
win has very little to do with me. It will depend on the

weather, people's whims, what they ate the night before, what they saw on the idiot box."

"If you feel that, then why are you making the effort, flying around, exhausting yourself, speaking to tree growers and grape pickers and experimental colleges? Why are you sitting up all night speaking into your machine and playing it back again and again?"

"Politics is an art to me. It is the only activity I have found that demands enough of my energies."

"You know, M said something like that once. Once I asked her did she hope people would follow her blueprint for a desirable world. She said she hoped they did, but if they didn't, she would have at least kept herself busy . . . Oh, Cameron, don't look so critical. I do wish you'd let us sit down just once and talk that whole thing through. I want to tell you about that week. About M, about Mike . . ."

"I'm sorry. I can't hear it. I can't hear all the details about how you got down on your hands and knees and scrubbed that creature's floor. Whether she was real, or whether you dreamed her up, the demeaning aspect of it is painful to me. As for any other . . . details . . . I consider them the necessary prelude to a miracle. Miracles should not be discussed like ordinary topics of gossip. I am a happy man, Francesca, a happy husband. I shall be a happy, devoted father. I'm no stranger to the old traditions, the old miracles, and I assure you I know how to conduct myself in the awesome presence of this one."

"It gives me the creeps, to hear you go on about this . . . miracle. Are you having a joke at my expense? I want to tell you the truth. I want to get it off my conscience. I want this baby to be treated like a human being, not some miracle."

Cameron got up from the bed. "I don't joke at your expense, Francesca. I am perfectly serious. I know the truth. You cannot tell it to me. As for the child, we will raise him."

"What if it's a girl?"

Cameron bent and brushed his lips over her hand. He had not touched her more intimately since their return. "Then she will be a beautiful one, like her mother. I'm off. I'm going to have another look at that house, then on to the golf course. I'm playing with young Freeman."

"It will be nice to have a house," murmured Francesca, moving her body to the left beneath the bedclothes, to follow the sun, which was slipping slowly, like a golden blanket, to the floor. "Is he the young reporter you stole from the newspaper?"

"I didn't steal him. He was looking for me, for someone to define him for himself. I like him very much. He is intelligent, he has ideals, and he recognizes value when he sees it. There's some fresh chicken salad for your lunch. I've chilled a bottle of Pinot Noir. We must get in the habit of drinking the local wines these next months. Take care, my love."

After he was gone, she thought about his body. It was becoming a mystery to her again. She went over the clothes he had been wearing today in her memory. The light slacks, the well-fitting black knit shirt. She could no longer see through his clothes to the shape of his body. Was it still as skinny? Somehow it seemed not to be. What if she found herself desiring him at some future point in their lives? Had she ever really had intercourse with him? She tried to remember what it had been like. She couldn't remember. All she remembered was that she had felt no passion. Why, what perverse thing in her, made her so certain she would feel it now? Because she knew he would never sleep with her again? Possibly.

He had insisted that she begin rubbing oil of almond on her belly at night, even though she was hardly showing. He didn't want a single stretch mark, he said. Last night she had asked him to rub it on her. Looking shocked, he had declined. He had said goodnight and retired to his study, where he now slept. She lay there alone and rubbed the oil on herself. Her tan was gone. The belly was slightly distended, not much, as though she had just eaten a big dinner. Through the closed door, she had heard his voice, talking against the background of Bach. She had not been able to tell whether it was his "live" voice or his voice on tape.

Now she looked at the other letter which had come in the mail. She did not open it. She knew what was in it. It was the letter she had written to M, apologizing for not writing sooner, apologizing for her desertion, explaining how she had every intention of going back, she had only meant to come here for a week and go to some dinner Cameron had his heart set on, and then she had gotten sick again. She thought it was the return of that mysterious virus that had struck her down in 311. No, it was the Miracle Virus this time. The doctor came. He poked and prodded and questioned gently. Tests were taken, confirmed. She had told Cameron, standing in front of him in the cold living room, forcing herself to look straight into his eyes, expecting him to strike her. He received the news with a long, inscrutable look. Then he had knelt down and kissed the hem of her dress. Before that time, he had slept in his study as a courteous deferment to her transitional emotions. He did not want to force her to do anything. He would wait, he said. The night he learned the news, he moved formally into the study.

She had not written M these details. She said only that there were certain junctures where things might have taken different turns. "If I had not gotten sick," she had written, "if it had not been the weekend, if I had not underestimated his terrible love for me and gone with him to the airport, if I had not agreed to come home and wear that dress 'just for the party.' As for the final If . . . well! I wonder how many women there are in the world whose stories would be different had it not been for *that* If!"

The letter to M had come back marked ADDRESSEE UN-KNOWN. This made Francesca smile. Then she frowned. Of course Cameron had seen it. He would take it as one more proof of her "imaginings." Did he really believe that? Or did he want to make her believe he believed it, to insulate her with self-doubts? Would she ever figure that man out? No. The thought did not altogether displease her. It gave her something to think about, to plot and plan for. People needed challenges, perhaps that's what Cameron meant about politics. She felt no passion for him yet, only a kind of fascination to see how far he'd go with this sacred mystery thing. If she found, at some future date, a wild desire to see beneath those clothes again, well, she would think of something. Maybe she would tell him she'd had a vision, God had spoken to her in a dream, commanded her to go to him. She would pretend the whole thing was torture. Yes, he would like that.

She often thought of Mike. She liked to think of him best in daylight, when the sun was shining. She remembered how he had looked as he sat in the airport, smiling, and how she had thought he was the type of person who could bring only good news. She thought of the sun-bleached colors in his hair and of the bright, daylight colors of that airport hotel room. She chose to believe the "good tidings" he had left with her had been planted in that first, bright room.

At night, he changed. Of course, thoughts were different at night. She was often by herself at night. Things grew cooler. She never liked to go into the living room when Cameron was out at night. She closed herself in the bedroom, turned on lamps, brushed her hair for comfort in the mirror, barricaded herself with magazines. When she thought of Mike at night, he became sinister. His face was always darkly in profile, as it was that last night when she had watched him sleep, when he had seemed such a closed country to her, the night she had spilled his cards all over the closet floor. Sometimes his face would disappear in slices, as it had that last morning when she had seen his reflection being shaved in the mirror. At night he still seemed a fateful emissary, but not one who came in spontaneous sunshine and joy. He seemed somehow in league with Cameron, part of Cameron's mysterious plans, "sent" by Cameron himself.

Did pregnancy weaken one's resistance to the old myths

and superstitions? She thought maybe it did. One *became* a myth at these times. Perhaps afterwards, she'd be better than ever, feel freer. Kate had given birth to a nine-pound girl. *When I saw the size of her, I was tempted to name her Brünnhilde or something. We decided on Diane, however. That suits a girl who will grow up running wild in the mountains. She is not a good baby, like you were. Already she shows signs of being a troublemaker.*

Francesca and Cameron had sent a gift. Cameron was very amused by the whole thing. Francesca had not yet told Kate her own news. She needed to grow accustomed to it, get her own feelings straight about it, this thing that changed her body, changed her life. She would probably not even tell Grace Fairfield when they went out browsing and talking together. Not at first, anyway.

She was already imagining this other woman, born on the same day of the same year. Where had she been born, in what part of the country? What had her childhood been like, what things had shaped her? Was she married, was she pretty, was she happy? At first, they would be formal with each other, not prying, each presenting her best self. Later, perhaps, they would become friends. Francesca hoped for a friend, another woman, someone articulate with whom she could discover herself.

She got out of bed and went in search of a pen, paper. She still had half a box of the stationery she had not given Kate. She found a fashion magazine to bear on, and returned to bed. But the sun had moved entirely off the bed and it seemed cool. Francesca slipped on her dressing gown and dragged a chair into the sun. She settled herself in, balancing the magazine against her knees. Soon she would not be able to curl into these positions. Her body would change, transform even as she watched it. She could do nothing to stop it. Nothing. The knowledge gave her a strange thrill.

"Dear Miss Fairfield," she began. Then paused. She crumpled up the paper and threw it on the floor.

"Dear Grace," she wrote on a fresh sheet. No. Not yet. She threw it away.

"Dear Grace Fairfield," she wrote quickly, with assurance. Then paused. "Thank you for your nice letter . . ."

She crumpled up this effort and threw it down with the others.

"Dear Grace Fairfield," she wrote, "I love your name. I think names are important, mothers should be so careful when they name their children. My name before I married was Francesca Fox. I was secretly rather vain about it. I liked the way it sounded. I thought it was an irresistible name. Your name makes me think of fresh meadows, fresh green things, fresh starts . . ." She paused and re-read what she had written. She frowned. She re-read it again, then crumpled it in a ball and got up from the chair with a sigh. She went to the mirror and sank down on the vanity stool with a sigh and brushed her hair. It had never looked better. It seemed thicker, sleeker. Jacques would marvel if he saw it now.

She wandered toward the kitchen, picking up her speed as she went through the living room. Everything was in place, immaculate. Cameron had vacuumed the royal blue carpet early this morning.

In the kitchen, she got out the chicken salad and a loaf of bread. Cameron had made some fresh mayonnaise. She poured herself a large glass of milk. It was too early for wine. She could hardly wait to get things arranged on the plate and start eating. Her changing body amazed her! Here she had scarcely finished breakfast and it was ready to go again. Perhaps she would give birth to a giant. She sat down, brushing her hair impatiently out of her eyes, and began to eat. The chicken salad was delicious. Cameron put nuts and black olives in it. She took a bite, another bite, greedily washing it down with the good, cold milk. Good calcium for the bones and teeth of a giant. She put away a hefty lunch, confident in the secret, rather sly knowledge that Cameron would never allow her to get fat.

For a complete list of books available from Penguin in the United States, write to Dept. DG, Penguin Books, 299 Murray Hill Parkway, East Rutherford, New Jersey 07073.

For a complete list of books available from Penguin in Canada, write to Penguin Books Canada Limited, 2801 John Street, Markham, Ontario L3R 1B4.